Please don't take Pride away . . .

Samantha opened the barn door, and Tor followed her in. "Pride's down here, just around the corner," she said, walking slowly down the aisle so that Tor could have a look at the horses they passed. She heard voices at the other end of the building, but that wasn't surprising. There would be grooms at work, cleaning tack and tending to other chores.

But as she rounded the corner, Samantha stopped dead in her tracks. Brad had taken Pride out of his stall, and a stranger was inspecting the colt. Pride skittered at the end of his lead and looked confused by the change in his usual routine. Brad jiggled the lead to get the colt's attention. "You can see he's got his dam's conformation," Brad said to the stranger. "He's been training beautifully."

"So I've heard," the stranger said, "but I'd like to see him work before I make any firm commitments."

He had to be the interested buyer Mr. Townsend mentioned, Samantha thought. Seeing the man's genuine admiration for Pride and knowing he could be the colt's new half-owner made Samantha feel sick. And she was furious. But Brad had every right to show Pride to the stranger. She couldn't try to stop him.

Don't miss these exciting books from
HarperPaperbacks!

Collect all the books in the
THOROUGHBRED series:

Also by Joanna Campbell

Battlecry Forever!
Star of Shadowbrook Farm

THOROUGHBRED

WONDER'S YEARLING

JOANNA CAMPBELL

HarperPaperbacks
A Division of HarperCollins*Publishers*

HarperPaperbacks   *A Division of* HarperCollins*Publishers*
10 East 53rd Street, New York, N.Y. 10022

Copyright © 1993 by Daniel Weiss Associates, Inc., and
Joanna Campbell.

Cover art copyright © 1993 Daniel Weiss Associates, Inc.

All rights reserved. No part of this book may be used or repro-
duced in any manner whatsoever without written
permission of the publisher, except in the case of brief
quotations embodied in critical articles and reviews. For information address Daniel Weiss Associates, Inc., 33 West 17th
Street, New York, New York 10011.

Produced by Daniel Weiss Associates, Inc., 33 West 17th Street,
New York, New York 10011.

A digest-size edition of this title was published by
HarperPaperbacks in May 1993.

First rack-size edition printing: November 1994

Printed in the United States of America

HarperPaperbacks and colophon are trademarks of
HarperCollins*Publishers*

10 9 8 7 6 5 4 3 2 1

WONDER'S
YEARLING

SAMANTHA MCLEAN'S HEART SWELLED WITH HAPPINESS as she studied the sleek chestnut yearling circling the walking ring at Townsend Acres. The colt's breath misted in the crisp October early morning air, and his powerful muscles rippled under his copper coat. He trotted at the end of a longe line around the perimeter of the ring for the training groom, his neck arched as though he was aware of his four admirers, who were standing at the opening of the walled outdoor ring beside the training stables.

Samantha's lightly freckled face was bright as she watched. The red of her shoulder-length hair nearly matched the color of the graceful colt in the ring. She turned to the colt's half-owner, Ashleigh Griffen. "He's looking good, isn't he?" she said, her voice full of excitement.

1

Ashleigh nodded and smiled. "And he's learning so fast! I really wish I could spend more time over here to watch his progress. I thought it would be easier now that I'm in college, but it's not. You're doing a great job with him, though, Sammy."

Samantha beamed at the compliment. She loved Wonder's Pride as if he were her own, and she was deliriously happy that Ashleigh had asked her to be the yearling's groom. She knew that Ashleigh still regretted that her family had to move away from Townsend Acres the year before. The Griffens had been the breeding managers at the huge Kentucky breeding and training farm for four years, but then they decided to buy their own small breeding farm on the other side of Lexington. Because there were no training facilities on their new farm, Ashleigh had to drive nearly twenty miles to Townsend Acres to visit her champion mare, Wonder, and oversee the training of her three-year-old filly, Fleet Goddess, whom Samantha also groomed and rode for workouts.

"I like the colt's movement," agreed Samantha's father, the assistant trainer at Townsend Acres. "Of course, I wasn't around to see Wonder in training, but I'd say Pride has his dam's potential."

"More mature than she was at his age," said Charlie Burke. The old trainer pulled down the brim of his battered felt hat to shade his eyes from the morning sun. It had been with Charlie's help that Ashleigh had transformed Wonder from a sickly foal into a champion. "Wonder had a rough first year—they didn't think much of her around the farm. It's different with this guy. Clay Townsend's maybe being a little too optimistic, though. This fella's got good energy and a nice straight leg, but no one will know if he's got Wonder's courage until he gets out on the track and into serious training."

"He's got courage," Samantha said firmly. "When he's in the paddock with the other yearlings, he definitely lets them know who's boss. No one pushes him around."

Charlie just scowled, but Samantha knew that didn't mean anything. The old trainer never let his real feelings show.

Samantha turned her attention back to the ring. Wonder's Pride was still striding easily on long, slender legs. Training on a longe line was important in teaching a young horse to walk, trot, and canter on command. From there, the yearling would be asked to do the same under tack, and then with a rider in his saddle. After that the horse would be taken out on the oval for more intensive training in preparation for competing on a racetrack.

The rays of sunlight slipping through the trees glinted off Pride's polished copper coat, accentuating the ripple of his muscles. With each bob of his

3

head, his silky mane flew. At a year and a half, he still had some growing to do, but already he stood close to sixteen hands. Samantha knew he was going to be a big horse.

"He's got all the right stuff, Charlie," Samantha called over to the old trainer, "and the bloodlines!"

"I've seen some perfectly bred horses that were flops at the track," Charlie answered.

Ashleigh shook her head and laughed. "Charlie, you're just itching for another star, and you *know* he could be it!"

"We'll see," Charlie said. "So, did you work Fleet Goddess on the Keeneland track yesterday?" he asked Ashleigh.

"I breezed her a half mile and galloped her out another four furlongs. She was raring to go. I'd say she's ready for the race tomorrow."

"Sammy and I are driving over in the morning," Ian McLean said. "You're welcome to ride along with us, Charlie."

"Yup. Sounds good. Saves Ashleigh from coming over here to pick me up."

"And if Goddess wins tomorrow," Samantha said, "it's on to the Breeders' Cup!"

"First she's got to win," Charlie reminded her.

Samantha didn't need to be reminded that there had been ups and downs for Fleet Goddess during the past year. The filly had started off her three-year-old season by winning two allowance races. Then Ashleigh had decided to point her toward

4

the Triple Tiara, a series of races for fillies held in the late spring and early summer. But during a workout in April, Fleet Goddess had pulled a tendon. The injury had kept her out of training for a month, and she'd returned to the track just in time to win the last race of the Triple Tiara.

"She's looked great in her last couple of workouts," Mr. McLean said, "and there's only one other filly in the field that has Goddess's class."

Ashleigh nodded. "I'm feeling pretty good about our chances, but I know I'll have a case of nerves by the time I get in her saddle tomorrow."

"And you'll forget all about them as soon as you ride onto the track," Samantha said. She admired Ashleigh so much. Her own dream was to someday get her apprentice jockey's license like Ashleigh. "They're finishing up," Samantha added as she watched Hank, the training groom, begin leading Pride toward them.

"He looked great, Hank!" she said, hurrying over to take Pride's lead shank from him.

The old groom grinned. "Sure did. I'd say you and Ashleigh have got something here."

Wonder's Pride butted Samantha with his nose. "Yes, you know you did a good job, and I'll bet you want your breakfast. You deserve it!" She smiled and rubbed a hand over the colt's soft muzzle.

"Maybe you could start working him in the ring yourself," Ashleigh said, appearing at Samantha's

5

side. "You must be learning a lot watching the training every morning, and Mr. Townsend won't mind. He's seen how good you are with Goddess."

"You mean it?" Samantha said, her eyes lighting up. "I'd love to work him, and Charlie and Hank have been giving me all kinds of tips!"

"I think it would be good for both of you."

"All right!" Samantha exclaimed.

"Well, maybe this colt will make up for some of the other setbacks around here," Hank said. "I heard some bad news from Tom at the stallion barn this morning. Townsend Prince slipped in his paddock early this morning and got his leg tangled under the fence. Looks like he may have broken it. They vanned him over to the clinic in Lexington."

"No!" Samantha and Ashleigh cried in unison. Townsend Prince had been retired to stud the year Samantha and her father had moved to the farm, but she knew his history and had seen the chestnut stallion out in his paddock. He and Wonder had raced against each other. Townsend Prince had been a champion in his own right, but Wonder had been just a little bit better, beating her half-brother in the Breeders' Cup Classic. The competition between the two horses had caused some of the animosity that still existed between Ashleigh and the farm owner's son, Brad Townsend, since Townsend Prince had been Brad's special horse.

Charlie scowled and shook his head. "Not good. He's turning out to be a good stud. It would be a sin to have to put him down. Townsend can't be happy."

"Well, I haven't seen him," Hank said. "He went straight over to the clinic when he heard the news."

"You think they might have to put him down?" Samantha said tightly. She knew as well as the rest of them the seriousness of a broken leg. Whether a horse could be saved depended on how bad the break was.

"They're operating on him, which is probably a good sign," Hank answered.

Mr. McLean ran his fingers through his auburn hair. "We'll just have to hope for the best. I don't think Townsend needs any more bad news."

"Not with the way things have been going the past year," Charlie added, "with auction prices way down and no decent runners to bring purse money in."

Pride tossed his head and nudged Samantha. "I guess I'd better get you back to your stall, boy," she said softly, her high spirits dampened by the bad news. "Then I've got to change and get to the bus."

Ashleigh gave Samantha a weak smile. She, too, seemed shaken by the news. "I'll see you at the track tomorrow, Sammy."

"Oh, my friend Yvonne is coming with us," Samantha said, trying to lighten the mood. "She just moved here from New Mexico this summer,

7

and she's never been to a track before. She loves horses and is really excited about it."

"She'll have fun," Ashleigh said. "See you in the morning."

Samantha started leading Pride toward the yearling barn at the end of the training area. The rolling green paddocks of the Kentucky breeding and training farm spread out around her, and sleek Thoroughbreds grazed on the lush grass. The leaves on the trees were just beginning to turn, and the white fences separating the paddocks shone brightly in the sunlight. At times Samantha couldn't believe how much her life had changed in the last year and a half since she and her father had moved to Townsend Acres. Until her father had taken the job as assistant trainer here, the family had traveled from racetrack to racetrack—wherever he could find work. The moving around had been hard on Samantha. She hadn't been able to make any long-term friends and she sometimes got lonely, but she had always managed to find happiness in being around horses.

Then her life had turned into a nightmare. Her mother, who exercised horses and helped with training, had taken a young, green horse out on a track for a morning workout. Everything had seemed to be going fine, when the horse suddenly spooked. He'd bolted with Mrs. McLean and crashed through the track railing. She was thrown through the air, and Mr. McLean knew as soon as he reached her side that she was dead.

Samantha still hadn't recovered from the loss, and neither had her father. Things had been getting better now that they were at Townsend Acres, but it was only gradually that they had been able to pull their lives together. Most of the people at the farm were great, and Samantha liked school and was making friends, although the previous year she had had to stand up to a few kids who had taunted her for being a "track brat." And, of course, she had the horses. She could shower her love on them and know she had their love in return. Samantha usually rode Fleet Goddess for her morning workouts, since Ashleigh couldn't always get to the farm, and every afternoon she went down to the breeding barns to visit Wonder. The beautiful mare was well cared for by the new breeding managers, the Lacys. She was healthy and happy and had a special place in everyone's heart, although they had all been disappointed that she hadn't had another foal. Twice she had been bred back to Pride's sire. The first time had been unsuccessful, and the second time, Wonder had miscarried. So for now, everyone's hope was on Wonder's Pride.

Still, even though Samantha was happy with her new life at Townsend Acres, she couldn't ignore the fact that things weren't going so well on the farm. And now there was the terrible news about Townsend Prince. The thought of putting down a magnificent animal like the Prince at six years of age made her sick.

"But I've got your training to look forward to, big guy," Samantha said to the chestnut yearling. "You're going to be great—I just know it."

Wonder's Pride snorted his agreement, then playfully lipped her thick red hair. Samantha brightened a little and rubbed her cheek against his silky neck. She led the horse into the yearling barn and down the immaculate aisle toward his stall. Other horses called out from their stalls, and Pride whinnied back. The air was rich with the scents of clean hay and horses and leather.

"Here we go," Samantha said as she led the colt into his roomy box stall. She'd already filled his hay net and water bucket. Now she took his feed bucket and went to the feed room at the end of the barn for Pride's morning ration of grain. After she'd measured it out, she brought it back to the eager colt.

Pride stuck his nose into the bucket even before Samantha had a chance to put it down. "Don't be so pushy," she said, laughing. "You've got all morning to eat."

The colt grunted through a mouthful of grain, and Samantha wrapped her arms around his neck. "See you this afternoon," she said. After giving his shoulder a last pat, Samantha let herself out of the stall and hurried back across the huge stable yard toward the small apartment she and her father shared. She quickly changed into school clothes, grabbed her knapsack, and took an apple out of the bowl on the kitchen table. Then she headed back down the long farm drive to the bus stop.

Forty-five minutes later, she filed off the bus in front of Henry Clay High School and hurried to her locker, where Yvonne would be waiting. Samantha had met Yvonne in history class the first week of school, when they'd been assigned to do a project together. They'd immediately hit it off, especially after they discovered they were both horse nuts.

Yvonne was leaning against a row of lockers, and she gave Samantha a wide grin when she saw her approaching. Her jet black hair hung straight to her shoulders, and her dark eyes were twinkling as usual. She had grown up in New Mexico and was part English, part Spanish, and part Navajo. Yvonne could speak some Spanish, and her great-grandmother had taught her a few words of Navajo.

"How did the workouts go this morning?" Yvonne asked. She was interested in everything that went on at Townsend Acres and thought Wonder's Pride was the most gorgeous horse she'd ever seen.

"Pride's training session was great," Samantha said, "and Ashleigh told me I could start taking him out in the walking ring myself."

"Hey, that's super!"

11

"Yeah, I'm really excited about it—I've always dreamed of helping out with his training. But there was some bad news this morning, too." Samantha looked sadly at her friend.

"What?"

"I've told you about Townsend Prince, Wonder's half-brother, right? He's one of the top stallions on the farm now."

"Right."

"Well, he slipped in his paddock early this morning . . . and they think he broke a leg."

Yvonne gasped. "That's horrible!"

"They've taken him to the clinic in Lexington," Samantha went on. "They're going to try to save him."

"It would be awful if they couldn't!"

Samantha nodded. She knew Yvonne shared her feelings about having to put down a horse. It would be a tragedy especially because Prince was a healthy animal. But horses were so dependent on sound legs, and they couldn't lie in bed, like a human, while a broken limb mended. They had to heal while standing on their feet, and sometimes they were forced to wear a sling under their belly to help keep the weight off the injured leg. Many horses resented the sling and couldn't adjust to a cast on their leg, so they thrashed about, often injuring themselves even more. "I hope I'll hear some good news this afternoon," Samantha said.

"So do I!" Yvonne said. Then, after a moment's

silence, she asked, "Is Fleet Goddess still going to race tomorrow?"

"Oh, definitely," Samantha said, "and Ashleigh said she had a really good workout yesterday, so I guess she's all set."

"Great. What time are you picking me up?"

"Eight thirty. Okay?"

"I'll be ready."

"I can't wait to show you around the backside, where all the stabling is. You'll love it!"

2

THE MCLEANS, YVONNE, AND CHARLIE ARRIVED AT THE beautiful Keeneland track in Lexington by nine the next morning. Mr. McLean parked in the lot by the backside, and they all headed out under the trees toward the rows of stabling barns.

They'd heard that morning that although Townsend Prince had broken a hind leg, the surgery to reset the bone had been a success. No one was overly optimistic yet, however. There still could be serious problems. Prince was going to be staying at the clinic, and all anyone could do was hope the stallion would improve.

"Hey, this place is big," Yvonne said as she looked around at the stabling and backside grounds. "And everything looks so nice."

"It's not that big compared to some other tracks,

like Belmont," Samantha told her. "But it is nice. Wait till you see the track clubhouse and the infield."

They wove their way between the shedrows. Dozens of sleek Thoroughbreds had their heads over stall doors. Grooms and hot walkers bustled between the barns, some carrying tack or feed, others walking or bathing horses. The air was filled with the sounds of horse calls, people chattering, and a distant radio tuned to a rock station.

Ashleigh and her longtime boyfriend, Mike Reese, were standing outside Fleet Goddess's stall. The big, nearly black filly had her head over the door and was watching the activity around her.

Samantha led Yvonne over to them and made the introductions. "This is my friend Yvonne Ortez. Yvonne, Ashleigh Griffen and Mike Reese."

Mike smiled. "Nice to meet you, Yvonne. I hear you're a horse lover like the rest of us."

"I sure am—though I've only ridden Western. Sammy's promised to coach me in English riding. What I really want to do is learn how to jump."

"Unfortunately, none of us are experts on jumping," Mike said, "but there's a good riding school not far from here."

Yvonne grinned. "I know. I'm already saving up my allowance money for lessons."

Samantha stepped over to Fleet Goddess and rubbed her hand over the filly's silky neck. Goddess was tall for a filly—over sixteen hands.

She had a beautiful, sculpted head with a triangular star on her forehead and the sleek build of a Thoroughbred in top health. "Hi there, girl. You all ready to race? I'm going to have you looking gorgeous—not that you look bad or anything."

Goddess whickered and nudged Samantha's hand.

"Sorry, no carrots for you now. It's too close to race time, but I'll give you plenty of treats afterward."

The filly pulled up her lip and shook her head in disgust, making everyone laugh.

"Your two-year-old all set?" Charlie asked Mike.

"As set as he can be. He's running in the third race. I'll be thrilled if he wins, but he needs the experience more than anything. I don't think he'll come into his own until next season. He's a little guy—not a big, strapping colt like Wonder's Pride. Ashleigh says Pride's coming along fast."

"He is," Samantha answered with a smile. "I think he'll be ready to race late next spring."

"Why don't you show Yvonne around?" Ashleigh said to Samantha. "We've got loads of time before Goddess's race."

"Sure. She's dying to see the rest of the track. We'll be back by eleven."

"Great."

The two girls set off down the row of barns. "The workouts take place early in the morning,

16

then the horses get walked, sponged, and fed," Samantha explained. "The races don't start until early afternoon." She led the way from the back-side to the oval of the track itself, with its mani-cured infield and sweep of grandstands. A work crew with tractors and harrows was moving around the track, readying the surface.

"Wait till you see the place this afternoon," Samantha said. "You won't believe how exciting it gets."

Yvonne gazed up at the grandstands, which were pretty quiet, except for a few track personnel pre-paring for the crowds that would arrive a few hours later. "I can't wait!" she said. "This is incredible."

The girls next visited the saddling paddock, and Samantha pointed out the walking ring. "That's where you really start getting nervous. You walk the horses there and wait for the jockeys to mount. I'll be leading Fleet Goddess later on, and of course Ashleigh will be riding."

As they came back through the barn area, Samantha showed Yvonne Mike's two-year-old, Moondrone, a compact little bay. Then they returned to Goddess's stall. The filly eagerly pricked her ears and pranced about the stall as Samantha un-latched the door and snapped a lead shank to her halter.

"Let's go for a walk, girl," Samantha said gently. "Keep you nice and limber. Then I'll give you a bath and a good grooming."

17

The next few hours flew by. The girls took a short break for lunch at the track kitchen before returning to finish Goddess's grooming. They gave her a bath in the sunlight, then sponged and dried her until her deep brown coat gleamed. They brushed her, combed her long mane and tail, cleaned her hooves, and then covered her with a light sheet.

By the time they returned Goddess to her stall, racing reporters and handicappers, who figured out betting odds on the runners, were roaming around the shedrows. Samantha nudged Yvonne when she overheard several of them talking about Fleet Goddess, and the two girls paused to listen.

"I'd put her in as favorite," one said.

"But she hasn't raced much lately."

"Yeah, but I liked what I saw in Saratoga—her last race. You want to put your money on that other filly, it's up to you, but I think you'll lose it."

Samantha smiled. "That's what I like to hear," she said to Yvonne. "Though some people are superstitious about their horse going in as favorite."

At three o'clock they all went to the stands to watch Mike's colt race and come in a fast-closing second. Then all too soon it was time for Samantha to change into clean jeans and the maroon and silver jacket bearing Ashleigh's racing colors.

When it was finally time for the horses in the eighth and feature race to be led to the saddling paddock, Samantha, carrying the filly's lightweight racing tack, went off to join Charlie, who was already waiting at the receiving barn with Fleet Goddess. Feeling butterflies in her stomach, Samantha motioned Yvonne to the side of the walking ring, where Mr. McLean and Mike were watching the proceedings.

Samantha held the filly's head, and Charlie fastened her saddle in place while a track official stood by and watched. Then Samantha began leading Fleet Goddess around the walking ring with the rest of the field. Her stomach was knotted with excitement and a little bit of fear, too.

"You're going to do great, girl, aren't you?" she said, rubbing her hand along the filly's neck. Goddess held her head up high, pricked her ears alertly, and gave a whicker of reassurance. "I guess you're not worried," Samantha said, "so I won't be either." A moment later she saw the line of jockeys filing toward the walking ring. Each wore the colorful and distinctive silks of the stable for which they rode. Samantha couldn't help thinking how great Ashleigh looked in her silks and shining boots, her helmet tucked under her arm. With all the hours she had to put into college, Ashleigh didn't have time to ride in enough races to qualify for her full jockey's license, but she already had her apprentice license and she looked just as professional as the rest of them.

Ashleigh and Charlie joined Samantha in the ring. Charlie was standing in as Fleet Goddess's official trainer since Ashleigh couldn't both saddle her and ride in the race. "I'm nervous, as usual," Ashleigh said with a wobbly smile, "but she looks raring to go."

"She sure is," Samantha said.

"I'd say she has her mind on business," Charlie added. "But I'd keep a close eye on the three horse. She'll be coming up on you fast with a late kick. Don't get caught unprepared."

Ashleigh nodded as she put on her helmet. Samantha glanced across the walking ring to the three horse, a dark gray filly, who looked calm and collected and seemed to have her mind on business too. When the call came for riders up, Charlie gave Ashleigh a leg into the saddle.

"You'll do great, girl," Samantha said, dropping a kiss on the filly's nose. "I believe in you. Good luck," she called up to Ashleigh.

"Thanks. See you in the winner's circle," Ashleigh said with a wink. "Okay, girl, let's go show them our heels."

"I don't know how you can do this all the time," Yvonne whispered to Samantha as the horses were being loaded into the starting gate. "My stomach's jumping all over the place. This is tension city!"

"You never get used to it when you have a horse running," Samantha replied in a low voice. "I felt the same even when my Dad's second-rate claimers were racing. And Fleet Goddess is really

20

special to me. There she goes—she's in!"

"Three more to go," Yvonne observed. "How long did you say this race was? A mile and a sixteenth?"

"Yes—and there goes the last horse." Samantha gripped her program tightly in her hand as she waited for the race to begin.

The gate doors flew open, and ten magnificent fillies roared onto the track. "And they're off!" the announcer shouted.

"Gosh, I don't think I can stand this!" Yvonne cried. "Where is she? Oh, there! Number seven. Hey, she's in third!"

Samantha nodded mutely. Her eyes were glued to Goddess and Ashleigh as the field swept past the stands for the first time and headed into the clubhouse turn. Ashleigh had Goddess on a tight hold back in third, but that was the way the filly had to be paced. Once she made the lead, Fleet Goddess tended to slack off and wait for other horses to catch her. Several times they'd caught her by surprise and cost her the race.

"That's it, Goddess," Samantha said under her breath. "Just lay back there nice and steady. Don't get rank."

"Rank?" Yvonne said. "What does that mean?"

"Fighting her rider . . . throwing up her head to get rein . . . but she's not doing that. Ashleigh has her settled in."

The horses raced out of the clubhouse turn and

down the long backstretch opposite the stands. The field maintained their positions, Goddess steady in third. Then the horse behind her started moving up on her outside, eating up ground. And from the back of the pack the three horse, who'd been last, started moving up, picking off horses one after the other.

"Charlie said to watch that one," Samantha said breathlessly. "Look at her go!"

"Why is Fleet Goddess still in third?" Yvonne cried. "The other horses are gaining on her!"

"Wait till after they come off the far turn. Ashleigh will let her out then." And Goddess had better have a lot left, Samantha thought, because the gray was moving up like a bullet!

"Now!" Samantha shouted as the horses came off the turn into the stretch. Then she saw Ashleigh slide her hands forward along Goddess's neck, giving her rein, and the filly responded with a kick, changing gears and gaining on the leaders with each stride. But the gray was still coming up fast. She was close on Goddess's heels as they both swept past the leaders.

"She's in front! Go, Goddess!" Yvonne screeched.

Samantha clenched her hands on the rail in front of her seat. "You haven't won it yet, Goddess. Don't back off! *Keep going!*"

She saw Ashleigh glance back under her arm. In the next second Ashleigh flicked her whip by Goddess's eye. The filly knew what that meant— the race wasn't over yet. Goddess gamely opened up a little more. And it was enough. The gray couldn't catch her. She flashed under the wire, the winner by a length!

"All right!" Samantha cried.

"She won! She won!" Yvonne shouted as the two girls hugged.

Mike and Samantha's father were grinning, and Charlie rubbed his hand over his mouth to hide his own smile. "Ash is going to be so happy," Mike said. "I guess it's on to the Breeder's Cup now."

"I guess so," Samantha agreed.

"Well, I'm hooked," Yvonne said. "Horse racing is fantastic!"

"Isn't it?" Samantha said, beaming. "And we have Pride's training to look forward to. Just think, next year I could be leading *him* into the winner's circle!"

Townsend Prince remained at the veterinary clinic all the following week. "So far, so good," Charlie told Samantha. "I hear if he keeps improving, they'll bring him back to the farm next week."

Samantha sighed with relief. She was so glad that the stallion was getting better. Things could have easily turned the other way, with such tragic consequences.

Pride's training was still going as smoothly as she had hoped. Every morning Samantha worked the colt on the longe line, having him trot and canter around her. The colt was eager to please

23

and quick to respond to her every command. Ashleigh came to watch and supervise when she could, and when she wasn't there, Charlie took her place, offering his expert advice.

The next Saturday morning after Fleet Goddess's race, Yvonne came and watched a training session. She'd spent the night with Samantha, and both girls were up at the crack of dawn to get Pride ready to bring up to the yearling ring.

Samantha was longeing him under tack for the first time that morning. She had spent patient hours in his stall over the last few days getting him used to the weight of the saddle, so he didn't balk in the slightest now. First she circled him at a walk, then gradually worked him up to a trot, and then a canter. He didn't need a whip snapped in the air to encourage him to change from one gait to the next. He responded to Samantha's verbal command. "That's it, boy, good; nice and steady," Samantha called out as she checked his strides for smoothness. By the time they finished the session, Samantha was smiling from ear to ear. Pride had performed beautifully.

"Good," Charlie said from the fence. "Stop him there on an up note."

Samantha signaled the colt to walk, then stop. "That's the way, big guy. I'm proud of you," she praised, gathering up the longe line and walking over to him.

Pride looked at her, his ears pricked at the

sound of her voice, then bobbed his head.

"And look what I've got for you," Samantha said, digging in her jacket pocket for the bits of carrot she'd stowed there. It was mid-October, and the temperatures were starting to drop. But they'd had a string of beautiful, clear-skied days, and Pride's training sessions hadn't once been interrupted by rain. "Let's go see what Yvonne thinks of you," she added, firmly patting his sleek neck.

"Not bad at all," Charlie said as Samantha and Pride walked up.

"He's gorgeous," Yvonne said with a sigh. "Especially when you see him moving."

"I suppose he's about ready to be broken to a rider," Charlie said to Samantha.

Samantha grinned. "Well . . . I was kind of thinking about trying to break him myself. I know I've never done it before, but Pride trusts me."

"I remember Ashleigh trying it on her own with Wonder," the old trainer said gruffly. "I caught her in Wonder's stall, standing on a stool, hanging over the filly's back. You *never* try to break a horse alone. Too dangerous—especially if you're inexperienced." Charlie pushed back his hat. "Well, if you're set on trying to break him, then you'd better let me give you a hand."

"Would you? Thanks, Charlie!"

"Better get him his breakfast first. I'll come down to the yearling barn in a bit."

As Charlie shuffled off, Yvonne glanced nervously

25

at Samantha. "I tried to break a green horse once—one of my friend's horses in New Mexico. The horse nearly broke me!"

"This will be different. I'm not going to just jump in his saddle. We'll go slow."

As Samantha spoke, Clay Townsend, the owner of the farm walked up. "Hello, Samantha."

"Hello, Mr. Townsend. How's Prince?"

Mr. Townsend gave his head a quick shake, and Samantha noticed that his expression was gloomy. "Too soon to tell, really. The vets have him in a sling to hold some of the weight off his cast, but I don't have to tell you it's serious. I went to see him today, and he's not comfortable or happy. We'll just have to see how it goes." His gaze swept over Wonder's Pride, and he seemed to brighten just a little. "He's turning out every bit as well as I thought. I hope he continues to, because we haven't had much luck with our two-year-old crop this year, and he's definitely the most promising yearling."

"I think he'll keep improving, Mr. Townsend. He's intelligent and really tries," Samantha said, running her hand over Pride's muscled shoulder.

"Good. I think Ashleigh will agree that we should point him to an early summer start next year," he said. "The farm's going to need a good runner. Well, I'll let you get him back to his stall." He patted the colt's neck, then headed toward his office in the stable complex.

26

"What did he mean?" Yvonne asked as soon as he was gone. "The farm's going to need a good runner? I thought Ashleigh owned Pride."

"Only half-interest. Mr. Townsend gave her half-ownership of Wonder after she won the Breeders' Cup Classic because Ashleigh did so much to turn Wonder into a champion."

"Boy, that was nice of him."

"Yeah, but if it hadn't been for Ashleigh, they never would have seen how good Wonder was. They were going to sell her as a yearling. Brad is still pretty ticked off that Ashleigh has a half-interest in both Wonder and Wonder's Pride, and now that he's out of college, he's at the farm all the time. Brad's always interfering in the training, and my father and the head trainer, Maddock, aren't happy about it. They say he doesn't know as much as he thinks he does. He bought a couple of two-year-olds at auction for a lot of money last winter, and they're duds."

"Why doesn't his father stop him?"

"Mr. Townsend isn't as involved in the training as he used to be. He travels a lot. Maybe he doesn't know what his son's like around the stables, and I doubt if any of the staff would dare complain about Brad."

Yvonne shook her head.

"Come on, I'd better get Pride fed," Samantha said. "Charlie will be down in a little while."

When Charlie showed up at Pride's stall,

Samantha already had the big colt fed and groomed. She'd also brought a bale of hay from the tack room and had it standing outside the stall.

"You ready?" Charlie said. When Samantha nodded, he turned to Yvonne. "Since you know something about horses, you can give me a hand. We may need two holding his head if he gets upset."

"He's not going to get upset, Charlie," Samantha said confidently.

"Better to be safe than sorry," he muttered.

The three of them went into the big stall, Samantha carrying the bale of hay. The colt whickered at all the company and playfully reached out and lipped Samantha's hair.

"Yeah, big guy. We're going to try something new today. It's a big step, actually." Samantha set the hay in the straw and rubbed a hand down Pride's neck and shoulder. "We'll go nice and easy. You know I'd never do anything to frighten you."

As she spoke, Charlie and Yvonne each took a firm grip on either side of Pride's halter. The colt snorted, knowing that something different was about to take place. "It's going to be okay," Samantha soothed. "Once you're used to a rider, we can really have some fun."

The colt flicked back his ears, listening to her voice, but he pranced uneasily in place. Samantha moved the hay closer to his side.

"You be prepared," Charlie said quietly. "If he

gets upset and starts skittering around, be ready to jump clear of his hoofs. He could give you a good kick without meaning to."

Samantha nodded. She stood on the bale of hay and gently laid her hands on Pride's back. His ears flicked forward, but he was used to the pressure of grooming brushes, and Samantha's hands didn't seem to bother him. After a moment, she gradually leaned forward so that more of her weight was on his back.

Pride snorted nervously, but Samantha continued talking to him in calming tones. "It's just me. I'm not going to hurt you. Nice and easy." The colt settled a little, although he wasn't entirely happy. Samantha now had almost her whole upper body leaning across his back. "Easy . . . easy . . ." she soothed.

His ears flicked back and forth, and for several moments, Samantha didn't move. She just let the weight of her body rest on his back. Then she lifted her feet off the bale of hay so that her weight was fully on his back. It was awkward, hanging over him on her stomach, and she just prayed he wouldn't suddenly spook and send her crashing headfirst over his side. She reached up with her left hand and wrapped her fingers in a chunk of his long mane to steady herself.

"You're doing fine," Charlie said. "You ready for him to walk?"

"Okay, big fella," Samantha said softly, "let's

just take it nice and slow." Samantha felt the colt hesitate, but he took a step forward . . . then another. She braced herself, half expecting him to suddenly start skittering around the stall. But he didn't. Soon they'd made a full circle around the big box stall, and Samantha was grinning.

"Okay. Try lifting your leg over him," Charlie said. "I'll keep talking to him." He laid an experienced hand along Pride's neck. "Yup. Let's just keep walking," he murmured soothingly to the colt. "Nothing to get nervous about."

Samantha took a breath, tightened her grip on Pride's mane, and heaved her right leg up over his rump. The colt started, but Samantha had already brought her right hand forward to grasp another chunk of mane, and her knees were tight enough on the colt's sides to balance her. She prepared herself for an explosion, and for an instant the colt shuddered.

"It's okay, Pride. That's a good boy. It's just me. Let's keep walking . . . that's it . . . good boy . . . you don't want to buck me off in the straw."

Pride flicked his ears and kept walking. They circled the stall twice more. Samantha couldn't believe her luck. He was accepting her! When Charlie and Yvonne brought the colt to a stop, Samantha leaned down and threw her arms around his neck. "Oh, you big wonderful horse!"

Yvonne grinned up at her. "Good going!"

Charlie pushed back his hat and nodded.

"Better than I thought it would go."

"Congratulations," a voice called from outside the stall. They looked over to see Ashleigh, with a big smile on her face. "I've been watching," she said. "He's got the same kind of trust Wonder has. It's great. Thanks, Sammy. Onward and upward!"

3

A FEW AFTERNOONS LATER, YVONNE TOOK THE BUS HOME after school with Samantha. The girls planned to take a ride on the trails, since Ashleigh had asked Samantha to take Fleet Goddess out to keep her in top shape for the upcoming Breeders' Cup races and Yvonne wanted to practice riding with English tack. She'd taken her preliminary test at the riding stable that week and was going to start lessons soon.

"The stable is great," Yvonne said as the bus traveled the country roads toward Townsend Acres. "They even have a huge indoor ring for when the weather gets crummy. I think I'm going to like it, but I still feel shaky with the English seat and the reining."

"Well, I can start coaching you this afternoon.

You ride Western so well that you shouldn't have any trouble learning."

"I hope not. So Ashleigh and Goddess are leaving for Florida for the Breeders' Cup next week?" Yvonne asked.

"Yes, and Charlie and Mike are going too. Goddess will be running in the Distaff, which is strictly for mares, but if she wins—"

"It'll be pretty fantastic," Yvonne finished for her.

"It sure will!"

It had been sunny and clear earlier in the day, but by the time the girls walked up the drive of Townsend Acres from the school bus, the sky had grown overcast. "I hope we can get a good ride in before it starts raining," Samantha said.

She led the way to the McLeans' apartment, where the girls quickly changed. Then they headed out to the stables to saddle up Fleet Goddess and Dominator, the old gelding that was used as a pace horse for the younger horses in training. Yvonne had only ridden in an English saddle a half-dozen times, but she'd barrel-raced out west and was a good horsewoman. What she needed practice on were the different techniques of English riding— the seat with shorter stirrups, requiring more use of the legs for balance, posting to the trot, and using both reins to signal commands.

They started the horses up the lane surrounding the paddocks at a walk, then worked up to a trot. When they reached the flat, grassy stretches at the top of the rise over Townsend Acres, they picked up the pace and began cantering. Fleet Goddess was full of high spirits and glad for the exercise away from the training oval. Samantha had to keep the filly firmly in hand, but Dominator was a steadying influence. The well-trained former racehorse wasn't bothered by much, even by an inexperienced English rider.

"Watch your hands and wrists," Samantha called over to Yvonne as they slowed the horses to a trot. "Straight out from the elbows. Keep your wrists firm. Okay, when you're posting, lift with his shoulder. Yeah. That's it."

Eventually the girls slowed to a walk. "Oh, I almost forgot to tell you," Yvonne said. "Bobby Perkins asked me if I was going to the Halloween dance today."

Samantha smiled. "Oh yeah?"

"He's so cute!" Yvonne said, grinning. "So I told him I was going. You're still coming to the dance with me, aren't you?"

"Sure. I told you I would, even though it sounds like you'll be dancing with Bobby the whole time."

"You'll be dancing too," Yvonne said. "Aren't there any guys in our class you kind of like?"

Samantha shrugged. "I don't think about it much. I'm friendly with some of the boys, but I'm not really that interested in dating and stuff, like a couple of the girls we know."

34

"You mean Janey and Rhoda and that crowd," Yvonne said, her eyes twinkling.

"Yeah," Samantha said, grimacing. "They act like jerks sometimes, giggling and flirting whenever there's a boy in sight. I've got better things to do—like train Pride and Goddess."

"That's true," Yvonne admitted.

"And Pride's doing so well! I rode him in the yearling ring this morning. He's really getting used to carrying me in his saddle."

The girls' cheeks were pink with color from the nippy air as they walked the horses down the last bit of trail.

"You're doing better every time," Samantha said. "You didn't neck-rein once today."

"Well, that's something anyway." Yvonne laughed. "I made lots of other mistakes!"

They were just rounding the corner into the galloping lane that led to the stable yard when the skies opened up. Cold rain slashed down on them in streaks. Goddess immediately shuddered in surprise. "Let's get them back quick or we'll be drenched!" Samantha cried, taking a firmer grip on her reins.

She set off at a canter, with Yvonne and Dominator matching strides. But by the time they reached the wide stable yard, they were soaked. They dismounted quickly and led the horses into the stable and out of the downpour.

Yvonne shook her straight black hair away from

35

her face. "Whew! Glad that didn't start till we were almost home."

Samantha pulled a towel off a tack box and wiped off her cheeks. "Let's dry off the horses fast," she said, "especially Goddess. I don't want her getting chilled. Dominator has a heavier coat from being out in the paddock."

They quickly unsaddled the horses, put them in crossties, and grabbed some more towels from the tack room. Samantha definitely didn't want to be responsible for Goddess getting sick just before the Breeders' Cup races.

A few minutes later they heard voices from around the corner of the barn aisle.

"How could you let them?" a voice cried angrily, and Samantha immediately recognized it as Brad Townsend's.

"I didn't have any other choice," answered his father's deeper voice. "They couldn't get him to settle. He kicked the rear of his stall and did even more damage to his leg. I would have waited until you got back from town and talked it over with you, but the horse was in too much pain. It would have been inhumane not to put him out of his misery."

"Why didn't they operate again?" Brad shouted. "There must have been something they could do!"

"The vet said the damage was beyond anything he could repair. Brad, I'm sorry. It's a tragedy, I know—"

Samantha looked at Yvonne in shock, then fell back against the wall of the aisle. They had to be talking about Townsend Prince!

"Prince was turning out to be one of our best stallions!" Brad went on, his tone echoing with pain.

"I know how you felt about the horse," Mr. Townsend said sadly. "You brought him along yourself—and this on top of the other problems we've had this year. Come to my office . . . we'll talk there."

Their voices ceased, and all that could be heard was the sound of their departing footsteps.

Yvonne gasped and turned to Samantha. "Townsend Prince was put down? Oh, no!"

Samantha felt numb. She couldn't believe it. Her voice came out in a hoarse croak. "Poor Brad." She'd never felt any sympathy for Brad before, but to lose a prize stallion and one so young, especially a horse you'd trained yourself—she knew how he must feel. "We'd better put the horses away," she said finally in a shaky voice. "I wonder if the others know yet."

The heavy downpour had stopped by the time they put Goddess in her stall and Dominator in the paddock, but there was still a fine mist in the air as they made their way back to the stable yard. The news had traveled fast. Already Charlie, Hank, Mr. McLean, and several grooms had gathered in the yard.

". . . a real shame," Hank was saying, "and Tom was telling me just this morning that he thought Prince would make it. This is going to hurt the farm."

Mr. McLean put his arm around Samantha's shoulders. "I can see you've heard," he said.

Samantha nodded. "Yvonne and I overheard Mr. Townsend telling Brad."

"The kid's going to take it hard," Charlie said. "That stallion was his pride and joy."

"Like the farm needs any more troubles," Hank added. "I hear the Lacys are moving on, too."

"The breeding managers?" Samantha asked in a daze.

"Yeah. Gave their notice to Townsend. Guess they haven't been too happy." Hank shook his head. "Sad day. I groomed Prince when he was in training. Got pretty attached to him myself."

"I guess we should tell Ashleigh," Samantha said, still feeling stunned. "Come on, Yvonne, let's give her a call."

A few mornings later, as Samantha rode Wonder's Pride in the yearling ring, she saw Brad Townsend watching them. He had been especially grim and short-tempered since Prince had been put down and hadn't spent much time at the stables. For several minutes he kept his eyes on Pride, leaning his tall frame against the fence posts. Then he scowled and strode off. Samantha didn't know what to make of it. Brad rarely came down to the walking ring to watch any of the other yearlings, and Samantha couldn't help but wonder if Brad was jealous that the yearling showing the most promise belonged to Ashleigh.

Then Samantha suddenly remembered that the Townsends owned half of Pride too, and the thought chilled her. Was Brad thinking of taking over Pride's training? She knew from her father and the other trainers that the older horses in training that year weren't much good, and that Brad always wanted the best horses for himself.

She felt even more uneasy that afternoon after school when she went to check on Fleet Goddess. Brad came up to her as she was brushing the filly in her stall. He leaned his arms on the top of the stall door.

Samantha looked over and waited silently. She had no idea why he was standing at Goddess's stall.

"So she's running in the Breeders' Cup Distaff," Brad said finally. "The only horse on the farm going, and she's not even one of ours."

Samantha still said nothing. She didn't know what to say, and she didn't like the sneering tone of Brad's voice.

"The next time you see Ashleigh, you can tell her she can start forking over some of that filly's winnings to pay for the accommodations we're giving her. Or she can find other facilities for her horse."

"She's paying for her own feed!" Samantha protested.

"Yeah, and she runs around this place like she owns it. Just tell her what I said."

"You can tell her!" Samantha fired back, but Brad was already walking off. She gritted her teeth angrily. "He always has to make trouble," she muttered to Goddess. Goddess gave her a sympathetic look, but now Samantha was too upset to concentrate on the filly's grooming.

She put away her brushes and hurried back to the apartment. She had to call Ashleigh.

"She has a late class today," Ashleigh's mother said when she answered the phone. "Can I have her call you when she gets in, Sammy?"

"Please, Mrs. Griffen, and tell her it's important."

Samantha went back out into the stable yard, feeling restless, so she went in search of Charlie. She found him in one of the tack rooms, talking to Hank.

"What's up, missy?" Charlie said when he saw the expression on Samantha's face.

Samantha's frown deepened. "I'm not sure it's anything, or if Brad is just trying to start trouble . . ."

"Most likely the latter," Hank said drily.

"He said to tell Ashleigh that she'll have to start paying the farm part of Goddess's winnings, or she'll have to move the filly."

Charlie shook his head. "As far as I know, she is paying Townsend something, but you'll have to check with her. I doubt that Brad knows anything about it, though, since Townsend senior handles all the bookkeeping."

"I just tried to call her, but she's not home," Samantha said. "The other thing . . ." she added, pushing her hands into her jeans pockets. "Brad was at the yearling ring this morning, watching me and Pride like a hawk. I know the farm owns half of Pride. You don't think—"

"I don't think the Townsend kid will interfere with the colt's training, if that's what you're worried about," Charlie answered. "Not yet, anyway. He has no interest in the early training. He only cares about the horses close to racing—and then only the ones showing potential. The kid's got no patience. He shouldn't get involved with the training at all."

"But there aren't any really good horses in training, and Pride's the best of the yearling crop."

"I still don't think you have anything to worry about. Townsend's pretty much told Ashleigh that he's putting her and me in charge of the colt's training."

Samantha felt a little better hearing that, but she still didn't trust Brad. She heard footsteps coming down the barn aisle and turned to see Ashleigh approaching.

"There you are," Ashleigh called. "I decided to come straight over here after class to check on Goddess." She looked at Samantha and seemed to

41

sense something was wrong. "What's up? Not more awful news, I hope."

Samantha quickly told her what Brad had said.

"I *have* been giving Mr. Townsend a percentage of Goddess's winnings—not because he asked, but because he's always been so good to me. Jeez, I know Brad's upset about Prince, but why does he have to start trouble with me?"

"Don't know why you're surprised," Hank said. "It's obvious that it bugs him your horse is racing in the Breeders' Cup. He doesn't like having Goddess's success rubbed in his face."

"I don't rub it in his face!" Ashleigh protested. "It's not *my* fault he hasn't got any decent horses this year—even if he did pay a fortune for those two colts!"

"I don't think he'll be buying any more," Charlie said. "Not this year, anyway. Money's too darned tight around here. Well, since you're here, let's go have a look at the filly. She's been eating like a champ and looks good to me."

"I want to go down and visit Wonder, too," Ashleigh said. "I haven't seen her in three days. She must think I'm deserting her. But first," she said, "I'm going to find Brad and set him straight!"

Ashleigh joined Charlie and Samantha at Goddess's stall ten minutes later. "Brad wouldn't admit he was out of line, of course, but I told him he couldn't get on my case about not paying my way around here."

After Ashleigh had visited Goddess and Pride, she and Samantha walked down to the breeding barns together to check on Wonder. Across from the barns stood the white house where Ashleigh and her family had lived for four years.

"I still miss it," Ashleigh said, looking over at the house. "I had a lot of great times there. My parents are so happy with their new place, though, and they've had a good first year."

"How could they manage to have a good year if the Townsends had such a bad one?" Samantha asked.

"My parents started out small. They bought some decent mares and bred them to good but inexpensive stallions. Also, they're not a training and racing stable, so they don't have the kind of expenses the Townsends have."

The girls walked to the paddock fence behind the stabling barns where some of the mares grazed. It was easy to spot Wonder. Her copper coat shone in the sunlight. Ashleigh gave a sharp whistle, and the mare's elegant head shot up. Her ears pricked in their direction, and an instant later she kicked up her heels and came cantering toward them. Several yards from the fence she slowed to a trot, then she slid to a halt in front of them, thrusting her head over the fence to nuzzle Ashleigh.

"Yeah, girl, I'm glad to see you too," Ashleigh murmured. "And I haven't forgotten to bring you carrots."

"She still looks like a filly," Samantha said admiringly.

"Well, she's not that old—only six. A lot of horses are still racing when they're six and seven. She would have raced another year if she hadn't injured her cannon bone."

"But then she wouldn't have had Wonder's Pride."

"Nope, so it wasn't all bad that she had to retire early." Ashleigh chuckled as Wonder reached her head down to lip her jacket. "Yes, I have another one in there," she said, pulling the carrot out of her pocket. "It's a shame she miscarried that foal this year. I think she feels left out watching all the other mares with their foals."

Samantha looked over at the paddocks where other mares were growing heavy with the foals that would be born that coming spring. The foals from the previous spring had already been weaned and were romping around in a separate paddock. "There's always next spring," Samantha said. "Anyway, I don't think mares should be expected to have a foal every year. They need some time off just to relax."

"I don't think Mr. Townsend agrees with you," Ashleigh said. "He's not very happy that she'll be going two years without a foal. Her foals are worth a lot—and right now, she's not earning a penny. I don't care, but Mr. Townsend certainly does."

"But look at all the money she's made already!" Samantha exclaimed.

"Right." Ashleigh smiled, rubbing Wonder's head. "She's paid for my college education and for Fleet Goddess, and someday there'll be enough to start my own training farm."

"With Mike?" Samantha asked a little shyly.

"We've talked about it. But we've got college to finish first."

"I'm getting so excited about the Breeders' Cup," Samantha said. "Do you think you'll finally get to see Goddess's half-brother?"

"Yes, Son of Battle will be there to race in the Classic. I'm really looking forward to the weekend. It'll be good to get away from all the rotten stuff that's happened this week. Oh, I forgot to tell you. Jilly called me last night," Ashleigh said, referring to Wonder's former jockey. "She and Craig are getting married in November."

"Next month? Hey, great!" Samantha said, grinning. "They've been going out a long time, and I always thought they'd get married."

"The wedding will be at her parents' place in Pennsylvania. It'll be small, just her and Craig's families. And then after, since they both have heavy riding schedules, she and Craig will be traveling around to different tracks."

"Did she say if she'll be at the Breeders' Cup?"

"No, she won't be there this year," Ashleigh said. "She doesn't have a mount."

"Too bad. I guess you would have liked to have seen her, but I'm sure there'll be a lot of other

45

exciting stuff going on down there," Samantha said, thinking about all the famous and talented horses, trainers, and jockeys who would be at the Breeders' Cup races.

Ashleigh smiled. "Oh, I won't be bored, that's for sure. Take good care of Pride while I'm gone, okay?"

"You don't have to worry about that," Samantha promised.

4

SAMANTHA WATCHED THE BREEDERS' CUP RACES WITH
Hank and several other of the stable hands on the
television in the staff lounge. Her father had gone
to Louisville for two days to race several of his
horses at Churchill Downs. He'd felt a little uneasy
leaving Samantha on her own, but as Samantha
and Charlie reminded him, she wasn't exactly on
her own, with Hank and other staff members
within easy call if she needed them. He'd offered to
take her along with him, but Samantha didn't want
to leave Pride for even a weekend. The colt was just
about ready to venture out to the training oval, and
Samantha intended to work with him every step of
the way. She also secretly relished the idea of being
on her own for several nights. She was fourteen,
after all—old enough for some responsibility.

47

She leaned forward in her chair and cried out with the rest of the staff as the field for the Distaff swept down the stretch toward the finish line. Ashleigh had rated Goddess perfectly, just off the flank of a long-shot speed horse named Lady's Luck, who had held the lead from the start. Lady's Luck had only raced on the West Coast, where she had a wonderful record, but no one expected her to handle well on the softer, sandier Florida track. Samantha knew that was what Ashleigh was banking on. She was probably expecting Lady's Luck to tire before the end, but Lady's Luck had ticked off slow early fractions—slow enough that she might have some gas left in her tank coming down to the finish.

"Go, Goddess!" Samantha cried as she saw Ashleigh give the filly more rein. As they pounded down the stretch, Goddess started moving up on the leader. Slowly, gradually she came up along the other filly's side. Samantha clenched her hands into fists and pounded her knees in excitement. The shouts of Hank and the other grooms echoed in her ears. "Come on! Get that filly!"

But Lady's Luck wasn't tiring. She was fighting back. The two mares came down the stretch neck and neck, nose and nose, lengths in front of the rest of the field. "You can get her, Goddess! Go! Go!" everyone in the room shouted.

The two horses swept under the wire. "It's a photo!" Hank cried. "But I'm sure our filly's going to get it."

Samantha hoped he was right, but she knew they couldn't be so sure. It was a head-bob finish, where one horse was lifting its head to gather stride and the other had its neck extended in full stride. Although Goddess had swept past the other filly a stride after the wire, Samantha was almost sure Goddess had been gathering stride at the wire.

"Be a pity if she loses it," someone grumbled.

For several tense moments they waited for the final decision. Then the results were at last announced. Goddess had lost by the barest nose.

Everyone groaned in disappointment, and Samantha expelled a long, shaky breath.

"Darn it," Hank said. "That other filly was setting much too slow fractions. That's the only reason she had anything left at the end."

"But what could Ashleigh do?" Samantha asked. "If she'd pressed the other filly and put Goddess on the lead too soon, Goddess might have started playing around and lost it anyway."

"Yeah, and the other filly's jock knew it," Hank said. "But she ran a darned good race. And Goddess still has her four-year-old season ahead. I think she'll do a bang-up job of it."

"I know," Samantha said, casting off some of her disappointment. Goddess *had* run an excellent race. She had shown heart, and there was always next year's Distaff.

*   *   *

49

As Samantha was leading Pride from the walking ring to the yard the following morning, she saw Mr. Townsend leave his office and cross the yard to his car. His shoulders were slumped forward and he didn't look happy. Hank walked up beside her.

"I hear he's headed to New York on business again," he said. "That means the kid will be in charge. Can't say I'm thrilled about it."

"When's Charlie getting back?" Samantha asked.

"This afternoon. I'm picking him up at the airport. Your dad's due back tonight too, isn't he?"

Samantha nodded.

"Well, this fella's sure coming along," Hank said, patting Pride's gleaming shoulder as Samantha untacked him. "If Charlie agrees, we can start working him on the oval tomorrow. Wish we had more like him. Townsend told me last night that he plans on auctioning two or three of the other better-bred yearlings we've been working with. And he's sending some broodmares and a dozen of the good-looking weanlings to auction too. Don't know what we're going to end up having to train next year."

Samantha had gotten used to Hank and Charlie telling her all the gossip, and she liked it that they didn't treat her like a little kid who wouldn't understand what was going on. "Well, we'll always have Pride," she said. "He'll be winning some purses for the farm and Ashleigh."

Hank laughed. "Confident, aren't you?"

Samantha's green eyes sparkled. "I think I have every reason to be. Right, Pride?" Then she grinned and reached for Pride's lead shank. "Let's go for a walk, boy. It's a beautiful morning, and pretty soon the weather's going to start turning cold."

"Yeah," Hank said. "Winter's just around the corner."

Samantha led Pride up the grassy galloping lane under the nearly leafless trees. The colt moved smoothly along beside her, looking curiously around him with an intelligent gleam in his eye. Samantha felt her heart beat faster just looking at him. "Guess what," she said. "Tomorrow morning I'll get to ride you on the oval. I can't wait!"

The colt nudged her shoulder and whickered.

Samantha laughed. "I can't believe how lucky I am. Everyone's letting me do so much with your training. I guess it's because Ashleigh knows how I feel about you. After all, she helped train Wonder when she was my age."

Late that afternoon, after Samantha had helped with some of the chores in the stable, talked to Charlie after his return from Florida, and paid a visit to Wonder, she went back to the apartment to call Yvonne.

"I watched the whole Breeders' Cup on TV," Yvonne said excitedly. "I had my whole family watching too, even though my brother was upset

51

because he wanted to watch a college football game. Football—yuck. It's so dumb. Anyway, for all his complaining, he started getting really interested in the races, and he couldn't believe that I had actually seen Goddess and was best friends with the girl who exercise-rides her. I was just so disappointed she didn't win! What a bummer! She should have won. She was in front as soon as they crossed the finish. She was definitely a better horse!"

Samantha laughed. "It's where she was at the finish that counts. It *was* a bummer, but I feel better about it now because everyone thought she ran such a fantastic race. And there's always next year. Did you see her half-brother, Son of Battle, win the Classic?"

"Yeah. He's something!"

They talked for a while longer, then Samantha hung up and gathered her books to finish her weekend homework. About an hour later, she heard the apartment door open and went into the other room to see her father entering.

She grinned. "Hi, Dad. Did you just get back?"

"A half hour ago. I stopped at the stables to make sure the horses were settled in their stalls." He came over and gave her a hug and a kiss on the cheek. "How was your weekend?" he asked a little worriedly. "Everything go okay?"

"Of course! How'd your horses do?"

He lifted his shoulders and gave a crooked smile. "A little worse than I expected. Tomboy managed a third, Orangeman a fourth, and Townsend's Mary never lifted a hoof."

"Sorry, Dad." Samantha frowned. "So, are you hungry? I was doing my homework and forgot all about supper," she said, going to the refrigerator.

"Go ahead and finish your homework," her father told her, going to the refrigerator himself. "I'll fix something."

Over dinner she told her father about her weekend, and they talked about the Breeders' Cup. But later, as they were finishing up, Samantha noticed him scowling.

"Is something wrong?" she asked.

"Huh?" He shook his head. "Oh, no, nothing for you to worry about. Have you seen my scheduling log?"

"I think it's on the table by the couch."

"Right," her father said, taking his plate to the sink. He retrieved the log he kept of all the horses whose training he supervised and went to the desk in his bedroom. Samantha shrugged as she took her own plate to the sink. Her father probably had some catching up to do after being away.

She fell asleep thinking about Pride's training session the next morning and was up before her alarm went off. She eagerly slid out from under her warm blankets into the still-dark room. After turning on the light, she quickly pulled on the jeans and sweatshirt that were hanging ready over the back of a chair, dug out a pair of socks from her dresser drawer, put them on, and drew her riding boots on over them. She saw, from the growing pile of clothes in her basket, that she'd have to do laundry soon. Since her mother had died, she'd had to take over a lot more of the household responsibilities.

As she passed her father's bedroom door, she noticed that he was still asleep. She went into their combination living room–kitchen, collected a bowl, cereal, and milk, and sat down at the kitchen table with the Sunday sports pages to read the recap of the Breeders' Cup races.

She was just finishing her cereal when her father emerged from his bedroom. "You're up earlier than usual," he said, noticing her empty bowl.

"I was too excited to stay in bed. Pride goes out on the oval for the first time today."

"Aha." He took a glass from the cupboard, filled it with orange juice, and took a sip. "I didn't have a chance to talk to Charlie when I got in last night."

"He and Hank agreed that Pride's ready," Samantha said, taking her bowl to the sink and rinsing it. Then she headed for the bathroom to wash her face and brush her teeth. She'd take a shower later, after the workouts.

A few minutes later, she was grabbing her jacket and running out the door. "See you outside, Dad," she called.

"Okay. I have a full schedule myself this morning."

The sun was just peeking over the treetops as Samantha crossed the stable yard, but already there was activity in and around the various buildings on the property. Samantha gave the other hands a cheery wave as she passed on her way to the yearling barn. Hank and several of the younger grooms were inside, just getting started.

"Morning!" Samantha called.

"You're here bright and early," Hank said, smiling. "I wonder why."

Samantha laughed. "I'll get him set," she said, moving toward Pride's stall.

"Charlie and Maddock want to get the yearlings out there before they start working any of the other horses," Hank told her. "The young ones will get too excited otherwise."

Samantha nodded as she went to Pride's stall. She leaned on the door and looked inside. "Ha! You're still sleeping. Lazy this morning, aren't you?"

The big colt had only been dozing, and he quickly came to attention, pricking his ears and letting out a soft whinny. He walked to the stall door and affectionately nudged Samantha's shoulder with his nose.

"Let's get you in crossties and give you a wake-up brushing," she said. "Looks like you gave yourself a nice roll last night." Specks of bedding were stuck to his otherwise shining copper coat. Samantha unlatched the stall door, took ahold of his halter, and led him to the nearest set of crossties. Grooms were leading out other yearlings and positioning them in crossties farther down the stable aisle. Samantha went to Pride's tack box, removed a soft brush, and went to work on his coat. She'd give him a more thorough grooming later, but a light brushing now would clean off the debris on his coat and stimulate his circulation.

By the time she was finished, Charlie and Maddock had come into the barn and were talking to Hank. Samantha saddled and bridled Pride. He took the bit without protest, knowing what it meant when his tack was put on—he was going out.

"We're going to have fun today, big guy," Samantha said. The colt snorted excitedly. "Hold on. We'll be going out in a second."

She saw Hank motion for them to start heading out, and soon Samantha and the other grooms were leading the yearlings across the stable yard and toward the training oval beyond. Pride pranced along on his toes, grunting in excitement. Near the oval, three of the regular exercise riders were waiting to mount the other yearlings. When the four grooms and horses stopped outside the gap to the track, Charlie came up to Samantha.

"All set?" he asked, giving Pride a careful once-over. "Colt looks like he's ready to go."

"He is. And so am I," Samantha answered.

"Up you go, then," Charlie said, giving her a leg

into the saddle. "Remember, we just want to get him used to the track this morning. We'll keep the four of them in a group and walk them first, get them used to going counterclockwise around the oval. Then, once they've settled in, we'll trot them, maybe canter them. See how it goes. Most important thing is for them to learn to stay toward the inside rail and not run out at the turns." Samantha nodded as she fastened the chin strap of her helmet.

Pride needed no urging to follow the other horses onto the track. There was a bounce in his walk, and he huffed out breaths of anticipation. This was something new again, and the colt was fully alert and interested.

Pride's smooth yet lively movements made Samantha feel great. She could sense the power he had yet to unleash. She moved Pride into position beside one of the other yearlings as the riders started the young horses counterclockwise around the track at a walk. Two yearlings were paired in front of them, and Pride didn't like bringing up the rear. He snaked his head forward and tried to nip the flank of one of the horses in front of him.

"Cut it out," Samantha told him. "You'll get your chance to be in front."

The rider beside her chuckled. "Showing his stuff already, is he?"

They circled half the track at a walk, then let the energetic young horses open up to a trot. Samantha kept firm pressure on Pride's left, inside rein to teach him to stay with the curve of the track and not run out on the turns. She also used the gentle pressure of her knees to help him bend, but he still tried to run wide around each of the sweeping turns, just as the other inexperienced yearlings in the group did. Samantha knew that only days of practice would teach them to stay close to the inside rail.

After another lap of the track the pairs switched— Samantha and the rider beside her moved their horses to the front. Pride seemed happier now as they lapped the track twice more at a trot, and Samantha marveled at the spring and energy of his step. *He's really going to be something!* she thought.

As they came around the far turn, she saw both Maddock and Charlie motioning for the riders to bring their mounts off the track. She reined Pride back to a walk and he obeyed, but the shake of his head told Samantha that he wasn't ready to stop yet. With the others, she rode through the gap to the grassy perimeter of the training oval where the trainers were waiting. Samantha saw Brad Townsend there as well, standing with his arms crossed over his chest and frowning thoughtfully as he watched the four yearlings come off the track.

"Good start," Ken Maddock called to his riders.

Charlie came up to Samantha and Pride and patted the colt's muscular shoulder. "Shows himself well," Charlie said. "Nice long stride. Looks like he was minding you."

Samantha nodded as she unsnapped her helmet strap and jumped from the saddle. She gave Pride another pat. "He listened better than even I expected. He didn't like being behind the other horses, though, and he wasn't ready to stop."

Pride had his head up and danced his hindquarters in a half-circle as Samantha pulled up the stirrups. The morning activity around the oval seemed to excite him, and his delicate nostrils were wide as he sniffed the air. Samantha noticed how the sunlight glinted off the muscles rippling under his copper coat. In her opinion, the three other yearlings couldn't compare to Pride. But of course, she was biased.

Then Samantha realized she wasn't the only one looking at Pride. Brad was still studying the colt, and his gaze gave her an uneasy feeling.

5

TWO WEEKS LATER SAMANTHA WATCHED AS YVONNE cleared a series of very low jumps and rode across the indoor ring of the Lexington riding stable where she took lessons. Since it was Friday, Yvonne had asked Samantha to come watch the lesson after school, and from there the girls planned to go to Townsend Acres, where they'd spend the night and Yvonne would watch Pride's morning training session. It would be his last for the season. Because he was still very young, it was important that he got a break from training so that he could grow and fill out.

The last of the six riders in Yvonne's class finished the round cleanly, after two tries, and the instructor called for them to walk their horses to cool them out.

"You're doing great!" Samantha said when Yvonne finally stopped in front of her.

"Thanks," Yvonne said breathlessly, "but we both know those were pretty easy jumps. And all the people in this class have ridden before." The other students in the class were dismounting on the opposite side of the ring.

Yvonne gave the gelding she was riding a pat, then dismounted and pulled up the stirrups. "You're no Wonder's Pride," she told the horse, "but you're not bad, fella."

"You've only been taking lessons for two weeks," Samantha pointed out, "so I think you're doing really well."

Yvonne shrugged. "I just thought it would go faster. I mean, I already knew how to ride."

"Yeah, I feel the same way about Pride's training—I wish that could go faster, too. He's been doing great—doing absolutely everything he should so far—but tomorrow will be his last day of training, and I'll have to wait until the middle of winter before we can start again."

"At least you can take him out for walks to keep him in top shape. Besides, we've got Thanksgiving and Christmas coming up. There'll be all kinds of stuff going on."

"Mmm, I know."

"Well," Yvonne said resolutely, "I've decided that by the time Pride is ready to race in the spring, I'm going to be good enough at jumping to enter a show."

61

"That sounds great!" Samantha said, laughing. "Then we'll both have something to look forward to."

As they spoke, Yvonne's riding instructor walked up to them. He was about sixteen and slender but muscular, with dark blond hair and blue eyes. "Hi there," he said, flashing a bright smile at both Yvonne and Samantha. "Yvonne, I just wanted to tell you that you're doing great in class. You're picking up jumping faster than the others."

"You mean it?" Yvonne said, beaming. "I was just telling Sammy that I didn't think I was learning fast enough."

"No, you're doing fine. Keep it up."

Yvonne smiled and tossed her head so that her black hair shimmered. "Oh, you haven't met my friend Samantha McLean. She's the one I told you about, who's been helping me with my riding. Sammy, this is Tor Nelson."

Tor gave Samantha another smile. "Nice to meet you. I hear you work with racehorses."

"Yeah. My father's a trainer, so I've been around Thoroughbreds all my life."

"I have a Thoroughbred myself," Tor answered. "And I'm definitely happy with him."

"Tor's one of the top riders on the show circuit," Yvonne explained.

He flushed slightly at her admiring tone. "I'm trying," he said. "Actually, a lot of the best

62

jumpers are Thoroughbreds. Some are retired racers, who only come into their own on a jump course."

"I've heard that," Samantha said, "though I don't know very much about jumping. I'll have to get Yvonne to teach me," she added with a smile.

"She'll be ready to if she keeps riding the way she is."

He looked over at Yvonne, and she blushed.

"Do you go to Henry Clay?" Tor asked Samantha.

"Yes. I'm a freshman, like Yvonne."

"I thought you looked familiar," he said, studying her features intently. "It's your red hair."

Samantha grinned. "People always recognize my hair. So you go to Henry Clay too?"

"I'm a junior. But I started late in the year, so you might not have seen me around school. My family moved down here from Maryland in October."

"Do you like Kentucky?" Samantha asked.

"So far. How could I not like being in horse country?" He flashed one of his bright smiles. "Well, I've got another class to get ready for. It was nice meeting you, Sammy. Yvonne, I'll see you here on Tuesday."

"You bet!"

As he walked off, Yvonne jabbed Samantha in

the ribs with her elbow. "Isn't he cute? I think he likes you."

"Oh, come on," Samantha said. "He was just being nice."

"Right." Yvonne's dark eyes were twinkling. "We'll see."

The two girls led Yvonne's mount back to the stable area. After they untacked and walked him, they turned him over to one of the stable grooms. Yvonne was still bubbling with excitement a few minutes later while they waited for Samantha's father to pick them up at the stable entrance. "Boy, am I psyched! Tor really thinks I'm making progress. I wish I could ride *every* day—but it's so expensive."

"You can always come over to Townsend Acres to ride," Samantha said. "We can go out on Dominator and Belle—since Goddess will be out in the pasture during the day for some rest time, and Pride's still too green to take on the trails."

"You don't think anyone would mind?"

"No, why should they? Dominator and Belle both need the exercise."

"It's a deal, then!"

When the girls got back to the farm, they grabbed a snack at the McLeans' apartment, then went to see Fleet Goddess and Pride. Since it was late by that time and Hank had already walked the colt, Samantha and Yvonne just fed him a few carrots and talked to him for a little while. Then they headed down to the breeding barns to visit Wonder.

The November afternoon had grown cool, and the Lacys had already brought the mares in from the paddock. Wonder was in her stall, cozy and covered with a blanket, but she greeted the girls with delight, whinnying and eagerly nudging Samantha for the carrots she knew Samantha had.

"I think Ashleigh and I have spoiled you," Samantha said, laughing. "But yes, I've got a carrot in my pocket—maybe even two." As Samantha reached into her jacket, Wonder bobbed her head.

"She's so beautiful," Yvonne said. "It's a shame you can't ride her."

"I know. I'd love to, but she's too valuable as a broodmare. It would be a disaster if she got injured. Ashleigh takes her out once in a while—but, of course, Ashleigh *is* her half-owner."

As Wonder happily chomped on her carrot, Jan Lacy came down the barn aisle toward the girls. "Hi there," she called.

"Hi, Jan," Samantha said. "You brought them in early today."

"Pretty nippy out. I can't believe it's the middle of November already." She stopped by the stall door and stroked Wonder's head. "I guess you've heard our news?"

"Yeah—I'm sorry you're leaving. It seems like you've been doing a great job."

"Thanks," Jan said. "It just wasn't working out the way we had hoped, as much as we love the horses. You know, we're originally from California. Our families are there—and, well, we've been offered a better-paying job on a breeding farm outside San Diego. So we'll be leaving in December—in just three weeks."

"Who's going to take your place?"

"I'm not sure yet," she said. "We've talked to Clay Townsend. He or his son will be interviewing."

"We'll miss you!"

Jan smiled. "We'll miss all of you, too—and the horses. We won't have a mare of Wonder's caliber to look after at the new place, but there'll be other advantages."

"Ashleigh was upset to hear you were leaving," Samantha said.

"Yes, I can imagine. She's like a mother hen when it comes to Wonder, but I'm sure whoever takes our place will take just as good care of her."

When the girls finally left the breeding area and headed back up the drive, Yvonne turned to Samantha. "The Lacys are really nice."

"And they're good managers, too," Samantha added. "Now I know how Ashleigh felt last year when she didn't know who would be looking after Wonder."

"Why doesn't she bring Wonder over to her parents' place?" Yvonne asked.

"Because Mr. Townsend insists that Wonder stay here."

As they walked through the stable yard they passed Charlie, who was just leaving one of the barns. "More trouble," he said, coming over to them. "Two more training grooms left today. They let one of them go, and the other one quit because he couldn't deal with the Townsend kid."

"Why did they let one go?" Samantha asked. "Most of the grooms are already real busy."

"Money's tight," Charlie said with a sharp nod. "They're going to be selling off some more stock, too, so maybe we'll get along fine with less staff." Charlie saw Samantha's expression and softened a little. "Now don't start fretting," he said. "Things aren't all that bad yet."

But more and more, Samantha could see that things weren't exactly good, either.

At dinner she asked her father if he thought there was more tension around the farm than usual. "Well, I've had some problems with Brad," he said. "While I was at Churchill Downs, he changed the training schedule on one of my horses, and did the horse more harm than good. But Maddock has had problems with him too. We'll work it out."

"Charlie said they laid off a groom today, and

67

Hank told me that they're going to sell more stock."

Mr. McLean smiled. "You're really up on all the gossip, aren't you? Well, let's hope it's just a little belt tightening. The stables will get by fine with a few less grooms."

Samantha wondered if her father was as unworried as he wanted her to think. When she and Yvonne were in the bedroom, with Yvonne in a sleeping bag on the floor, Samantha lay staring up at the ceiling, deep in thought. "You know," she said to her friend, "everything's been so good since we moved here. I've been so happy staying in one place and not moving around all the time like we used to. I should have known things couldn't stay that way."

"What makes you think things are going to change?" Yvonne asked.

"I don't know. I don't like all this bad stuff we've been hearing."

"Oh, Samantha. You worry too much."

Charlie was waiting by the oval the next morning when the girls brought up Wonder's Pride. Farther up the oval rail, Mr. McLean and Maddock were readying the horses they would be working. Samantha also spotted Brad there, standing a head taller than the exercise riders next to him, and not far from him was Mr. Townsend. It looked like everyone would be watching Pride's last training session of the season.

In the past two weeks of daily workouts, the yearlings had become accustomed enough to the track that they could be worked in pairs. Samantha—under Ashleigh's or Charlie's supervision—had patiently increased the distance and pace of Pride's workouts. He now jogged the full mile of the track and finished up with a short gallop.

Even though the workouts weren't demanding, Samantha knew that Pride shone in comparison to the other yearlings in training. There was something special about the way he carried himself, and he drew people's attention. Samantha had noticed how frequently admiring gazes lingered on him. The colt was really going to be something.

Charlie walked over to Pride, Samantha, and Yvonne. "Mornin'," he said, quickly checking Pride's girth.

"He couldn't wait to get out here," Samantha told Charlie, zipping up her down vest against the chill in the air.

"Well, let's get started, then." He gave Samantha a leg into the saddle as Ashleigh held the colt's head. Before Samantha had even settled herself, Pride began prancing restlessly beneath her. She quickly fastened her chin strap and gathered up the reins.

"You know what to do," Charlie said. "After

they're warmed up, jog him a mile, then let him out to a gallop for another half." He glanced over to Maddock, who had just finished talking to Johnny Byard, the exercise rider on one of the other yearlings. Maddock gave both the rider and Charlie a nod. "Go to it," he told Samantha.

Pride trotted briskly forward as soon as Samantha touched him with her heels. They moved with the other horse and rider through the gap. "I hope we can keep up with you," Johnny told Samantha. "He looks like he's full of go."

"Don't worry, I won't be letting him out all the way."

They set off at a trot to warm up the horses. At the half-mile marker pole, they exchanged a glance and simultaneously urged both of the young horses into a canter. Both horses changed stride smoothly and cantered on the correct leads, striking out with their inside foreleg so that they were properly balanced as they circled the track.

Stride for stride the two horses jogged the oval. Samantha relaxed into the rocking gait, half standing in the stirrups. She kept her eyes focused ahead, relishing the feel of the powerful young horse and the crisp morning breeze on her face.

When they'd lapped a mile, the two riders exchanged another glance and nod. Then Samantha crouched lower in the saddle and slid her hands along Pride's muscular neck. "Okay, boy, let's gallop!"

The colt took off, quickly settling into a collected gallop. Pride's movements felt effortless to Samantha, but she could tell the colt beside them wasn't having as easy a time of it.

The wind whipped Pride's long mane into Samantha's face. Her ears echoed with the rhythmic pound of hoofbeats and the horses' snorted breaths. The horses roared around the far turn, and too soon the marker pole loomed in the distance. They flashed by it, and both riders immediately stood in their stirrups and drew back on the reins, signaling the horses to slow, first to a canter, then a trot. Then they turned the horses and headed back to the gap.

Samantha proudly patted Pride's arched neck. "Good boy. That's the way to go!" He tossed his head in acknowledgment and lifted his feet even higher as they trotted over the harrowed dirt.

"I think he's going to be a winner," Johnny called over to her. "He could have had us beat and he wasn't even trying."

Samantha grinned. "He's something, all right!"

Her face was glowing as they joined the crowd of trainers and riders. Mr. Townsend looked pleased, and everyone was smiling—except for Brad, who was just staring at Pride. Samantha's father gave her a thumbs-up as Charlie came over to take Pride's head.

"Looks like he came out of it just fine," Charlie said, giving the colt a once-over.

Samantha dismounted and Yvonne hurried over. "Do you know how great you two looked out there?" Yvonne asked.

"I had a feeling," Samantha said, almost bursting with happiness. She turned to Pride. "We're going places, big guy."

He bobbed his head, and Samantha laughed.

6

ON A CRISP AFTERNOON IN MID-DECEMBER, WHEN Samantha was on her way to visit Wonder, Horace Johnston, the new breeding manager, came out of his office and into the barn aisle. It was the first time she'd ever seen him, although she knew he'd been interviewed and hired by Brad since Mr. Townsend was away on another business trip. He was a big man in his fifties, whose thinning hair was slicked down to his head, and though Samantha didn't think he was exactly sloppy, there was something unkempt about his appearance.

She smiled in a friendly way when he crossed her path and started to say hello, but Johnston gave her a cold look, then strode right on past her.

A second later Bill Parks, who worked in the

73

breeding barns, came up behind Samantha. "Friendly character, isn't he?" Bill said drily.

Samantha closed her gaping mouth. "Is he that way to everyone?"

"He's not the most pleasant person I've ever met."

"Is he all right with the horses?" Samantha asked with alarm.

Bill fingered his chin thoughtfully. "Haven't seen him do anything wrong, but he doesn't handle the horses much himself. He pretty much leaves that to me and the undergrooms."

Samantha thought that was strange. She knew the Griffens and the Lacys had always taken a very active part in handling the horses in their charge.

Bill Parks seemed to be reading her thoughts. "Everybody's different," he said, shrugging. But Samantha could see from his expression that he wasn't very happy with the new situation.

She walked on to Wonder's stall deep in thought. Maybe Johnston *was* cold and unfriendly, but if he did his job well, then she shouldn't worry. Besides, she knew Bill would keep his finger on everything.

As Christmas approached, Samantha visited the mares' barn every few days. She saw Mr. Johnston a couple of times, and even though he hadn't done anything to make her suspicious, she couldn't help but think there was something sneaky, even dishonest about him.

Whenever the weather was decent, Samantha took Pride for long walks over the farm trails, and Yvonne came over frequently. The two girls often went riding on Dominator and Belle, since Goddess and Pride had the winter off. Then there was Christmas shopping to do, and Ashleigh drove Samantha into Lexington so they could spend a day in the stores.

The weekend before, Samantha and Yvonne had gone to the big, all-high-school Christmas dance, and Tor Nelson had been there. Samantha had bumped into him in the school hallways a few times, but since they were in different classes, she hadn't really had a chance to talk to him. On the night of the dance he came over to talk to Samantha, Yvonne, and Bobby Perkins, and later he and Samantha had danced. She had really enjoyed herself. Tor had a good sense of humor, but more important, he was genuinely interested in what mattered most to Samantha—horses.

On Christmas Day, the smells of roasted turkey and pine filled the Griffen house. The Griffens had invited Charlie and the McLeans over for a special dinner. Mike and his father were there too, of course, and so were Ashleigh's brother and sister, Rory and Caroline, and Caroline's longtime boy-friend, Jason.

By the time dinner was ready to be served, everyone was cheerful, chattering and laughing as they took their seats at the table. Not surprisingly, the Thoroughbred industry was the main topic of conversation throughout the meal. Mr. and Mrs. Griffen talked a little about the first year on their farm, and fourteen-year-old Rory, who was taking a real interest in the business, glowingly described the first crop of weanlings.

"Maybe you're exaggerating just a little, Rory," Mr. Griffen said, laughing. "So, what do you think of the new breeding manager at Townsend Acres?" he asked the others.

"I don't have much contact with him, but he strikes me as a hard man to get to know," Samantha's father told him. "He really keeps to himself."

"Well, I don't like him at all," Samantha said bluntly, glancing across the table at Ashleigh. Samantha knew Ashleigh shared her feelings about Horace Johnston.

"I don't like him either," Ashleigh agreed.

"You two have some pretty strong reactions," Mr. Reese said. "Why? Is he neglecting the horses?"

"I haven't seen any signs of *that*," Samantha admitted, "but Bill does most of the work. Johnston doesn't seem very interested in the horses. I wonder sometimes if he even likes them."

"But so far he's doing his job, so you can't point the finger at him," Charlie said.

Mr. Griffen helped himself to more turkey. "I can't see Townsend keeping on a breeding manager who isn't up to snuff, though I hear things are pretty tight over there."

"They could be better," Mr. McLean admitted. "They're going to be selling more broodmares and some good weanlings at the Keeneland auction next month. And some of the yearlings that started training this fall will be going too. They've also let a few training grooms go and haven't rehired."

"Yup," Charlie said brusquely. "And Townsend's too preoccupied with money troubles to pay much attention to the training, and his kid's got everybody's back up. He walks around checking up on you, putting his two cents in—as if we haven't been running a good training stable for years without his help."

Mr. McLean nodded grimly. "At least he hasn't interfered with any of your horses, Charlie."

"Nope, and he'd better not. We've got Wonder's colt coming along."

"Ashleigh tells me he's doing well," Mr. Griffen said.

"He is, though it's kind of soon to start counting chickens. We'll see how he does in February when he goes back into training."

The conversation then turned to Fleet Goddess, who would go back in training in February too. Samantha was glad for the change in conversation. She didn't like all the gloomy talk about Townsend Acres, even if it was true.

"Oh, I got a Christmas card from Jilly," Ashleigh

announced. "She and Craig will both be riding this winter at Aqueduct. She sounds really happy."

"Got a card from her myself," Charlie said. "Glad that things are working out so well for her."

"I miss not having her around," Ashleigh added, "but as long as she's happily married now . . ."

"That's all that counts," Charlie said.

After dinner, everyone moved to the living room to have coffee and dessert. Ashleigh and Samantha went to sit together on the floor in front of the fire, which was blazing on the hearth. "I'm so glad it's midterm break," Ashleigh said. "Now I'll have more time to get over to Townsend Acres. I feel like I've been neglecting Wonder and Goddess and Pride."

"And Pride's really filling out," Samantha said. "I think he's grown another inch in the last month!"

Ashleigh smiled. "What does that make him? Close to seventeen hands?"

"Almost."

"By the way, how's your friend Yvonne doing? Did she start riding lessons yet?"

"Oh yeah, and she loves it. I'm going into Lexington on Tuesday to watch her class. And she'll probably ride with me at the farm a few times over our vacation."

Caroline and Jason came over and joined them by the fireplace, and Caroline eagerly talked about her and Jason's plans for after their graduation from college in the spring. They both planned on staying in Louisville and were already looking for jobs.

Samantha was tired when she, her father, and Charlie pulled into Townsend Acres.

"Nice party," Charlie said gruffly. "I suppose you'll be going out to see the horses now," he said to Samantha.

"Goddess and Pride, anyway. Ashleigh and I went down to see Wonder this morning."

"Guess I'll go with you," the old trainer said.

"Then I'll come too," Mr. McLean volunteered. "I've always enjoyed giving my horses a little Christmas treat."

Samantha had already stashed some carrots and apples in the stable, and the three of them went from stall to stall, rationing out goodies to each of the horses. It was close to midnight when they finally finished making the rounds.

What a wonderful way to end Christmas, Samantha thought as she, her father, and Charlie headed to their apartments in the cold, starlit night. "Merry Christmas, Charlie!" she called as they parted ways.

"Yup," said the old trainer. "Same to you both."

When they were inside, Samantha's father handed her a small box. "I thought I'd save this for last," he said.

Samantha held the velvet box in her hand for a moment, staring at it. She and her father had already

exchanged presents that morning, and she wondered what this extra present could be. She flipped
open the lid and saw a pair of pearl stud earrings.
She gasped with surprise.

"They were your mother's," her father said. "I
wanted to wait until you could really appreciate
them. I think you're old enough now."

Samantha felt the hot sting of tears in her eyes.
She threw her arms around her father. "Thank you,
Dad!"

"You're very welcome, sweetheart."

Samantha was up at dawn every morning that
week even though she was on vacation. After
breakfast each day, she groomed Goddess and
Pride, then she helped with some other chores
around the stables, since the farm was short on
staff. On Tuesday her father dropped her off at
Yvonne's riding stable. "I'll pick you up in about
two hours, after I run some errands and go to the
tack and feed store," he said.

He was frowning, and Samantha knew he was
annoyed because several of the errands he was
running were for Brad. It definitely wasn't part of
his job to be an errand boy, but with the staff cut
back, he didn't have much choice.

Yvonne was already mounted and waiting for
the class to begin. She waved as Samantha took a
seat on the small set of bleachers at one end of the
ring.

Tor saw Samantha too, and he gave her a wide smile before walking to the center of the ring and calling the class to order. The class started warming up their horses by trotting and cantering in circles and figure eights up and down the length of the huge ring. From there they progressed to several low warm-up jumps——crossbars and single rails. Tor was a good instructor, Samantha noticed. He was patient with the students who were having trouble, yet firm in correcting them. Samantha also noticed that Yvonne excelled over the rest of the class. She had a natural grace and balance in the saddle now that she had a firm grasp of the techniques of English riding, and she had good communication with her mount. She didn't confuse him with mixed and awkward signals, and the horse responded.

Tor then set up a series of small jumps on the perimeter of the ring. None of the jumps were especially high—three feet at the most—but they were varied. There was a crossbar, a small parallel, a low gate, and a combination rail and brush. They were spaced at different intervals, forcing the rider to adjust the horse's stride in order to meet each jump properly. Half of the six students in the class faltered, and their mounts refused jumps.

"You need more leg," Tor instructed one patiently. "You came up to that jump a half-stride off." Then he had the rider try the jump again.

But Yvonne went through the series on her first

try without a problem. Samantha smiled as Tor praised her friend.

At the end of the lesson, as the class walked their horses around the ring to cool them out, Tor came over to Samantha. "I'm glad you came by," he said. "Yvonne's doing great, isn't she?"

"Incredible. And you're a good teacher."

He flushed. "Thanks. It's hard sometimes not to lose it with some of them. But this class is pretty good. How's your vacation going?"

"Okay—I'm having fun," Samantha said. "But I'm looking forward to training starting up again in February."

"That's when I'll start some heavy-duty training too," Tor said. "I'll be getting ready for the spring and summer shows. Have you seen my gelding?"

"No, but Yvonne's told me about him. She says he's a pretty spectacular jumper."

"He is," Tor answered proudly. "He wouldn't win any beauty contests, but he's some athlete. Why don't you come and take a look at him after class? I have a few minutes before the next group arrives."

"Sure, I'd love to."

A few minutes later, Tor signaled the class to take their horses back to the stable, and he and Samantha followed. As they passed Yvonne Samantha called, "You looked great! I'll see you in a few minutes. I'm going to see Tor's horse."

82

"Okay, I'll meet you in the stables," Yvonne called back.

Tor led Samantha to a wing of the stables reserved for privately owned horses. Elegant heads poked over the stall doors, watching them as they walked by. Tor stopped at a stall marked with a brass nameplate that said TOP HAT.

The Thoroughbred gelding was big and almost pure white, but Samantha could see what Tor meant about him not winning beauty contests. His ears were oversize, and his nose was oddly shaped. But he definitely had the build of a jumper, with muscular hindquarters that would send him soaring.

"How did you find him?" Samantha asked.

"Through friends in the jumping circuit," Tor said. "They'd bought him at auction and had started training him. He had early training as a racehorse, but I don't know if he ever made it to the track. His bloodlines showed that he could have real jumping potential, and he did."

"How old is he?"

"Eight—not very old for a top-class jumper. Most of them don't hit their prime until they're twelve or so."

Just then Yvonne joined them, looking incredibly cheerful after her good lesson. "You should see Top Hat jump," she said to Samantha. "He makes it look so effortless, like he has wings or something."

"He loves it," Tor said. "That makes all the difference." He glanced at his watch. "I'd better go. My next class will be starting soon. Come and watch the class anytime," he said to Samantha.

"I will."

"I'll see you in school next week."

As he hurried off, Yvonne gave Samantha an exaggerated wink. "I wonder when he'll ask you out."

"Don't start," Samantha said, then laughed.

Over the next few weeks, the cold January weather and frozen ground forced everybody inside. Samantha kept busy in the afternoons grooming Goddess and Pride, and each day she went down to visit Wonder.

But the more she saw of the new breeding manager, the more uneasy she felt. She began to notice that Johnston was away from his office more than he was in it, and he certainly didn't seem to be spending much time tending to duties around the barns. With the cold weather and icy pastures, most of the mares were kept in their stalls, but they needed exercise, and Samantha rarely saw Johnston leading them out for walks.

Then, in mid-January, Bill Parks quit.

"I hate to go," he told Samantha, "but it's just not working out between me and Johnston. I'm going over to Gainesway. They made me an offer I couldn't refuse."

Samantha knew Gainesway was as big an operation as Townsend Acres, but what would happen without Bill to keep an eye on Johnston?

All the staff in the training area were upset about the news, especially because there was no sign that a replacement was going to be hired. The only two grooms left in the breeding barns shook their heads wearily when Ashleigh asked them what was going on.

"I don't see him interviewing anyone, and the two of us just can't get everything done," Petie Forman told Ashleigh as Samantha looked on. "I've been here for two years, and I've loved every minute of it. Micky's liked working here too, but we need help. We run our legs off all day, and Johnston never lifts a finger. Half the time he's out back in the storage room with his *Racing Form*."

Considering what the groom had said, Samantha wasn't surprised that the barns weren't as well kept as they'd once been. Bits of hay littered the aisles that should have been hosed down every morning, and the horses' stalls were mucked out far less frequently. In fact, one afternoon Samantha had grabbed a pitchfork and cleaned Wonder's stall herself because it hadn't been mucked out properly.

Johnston walked up just as she was finishing. "What do you think you're doing?" he asked her coldly.

"Her stall was dirty," Samantha said. "So I cleaned it."

85

"I run this operation," Johnston snapped, "and I don't need a know-it-all kid interfering."

"I'm *not* interfering," Samantha shot back.

Johnston didn't respond, but his expression was ugly as he strode off down the aisle.

"He's awful!" Samantha growled to Wonder. "He shouldn't be working here. I think I should talk to Mr. Townsend."

Samantha was too angry to consider what Mr. Townsend might think of her making complaints when she was only the assistant trainer's daughter. She found him in his office, and he motioned her in when she said she needed to talk to him. But as she explained to him the situation in the breeding barns, he seemed distracted and only half listening.

"I'll go down and take a look," he told her when she'd finished. "Or I'll send Brad down. I've more or less put him in charge of overseeing things. We're trying to cut the staff until things pick up, but I don't want to see the horses neglected, either."

Samantha bit her tongue until she had left his office. *He's put* Brad *in charge of overseeing things?* she thought. *A lot of good that will do*.

Much later that afternoon Samantha saw Mr. Townsend and Brad head down to the breeding area. Curiosity got the best of her and she decided to follow the two men into the barn. She looked in through a crack in the barn door, and her eyes widened. The place was suddenly immaculate—not a single piece of straw littered the aisle. And Johnston was talking to Mr. Townsend in eager, fawning tones.

Someone *had* to have told him the Townsends were coming. That was the only explanation. Samantha knew he wouldn't have cleaned up the barn otherwise. She huffed out a frustrated sigh. The Townsends would think she was a trouble-maker. They would never believe her if she told them the barn had looked much different two hours earlier.

She walked back up to the training area in disgust. Once the Townsends were gone, Samantha was sure Johnston would slip right back into his lazy habits. Maybe Ashleigh could help, she thought. She'd have to call and tell her the bad news.

7

THE NEXT MORNING, SAMANTHA DISCOVERED THE REASON for Johnston's sudden clean-up. He *had* known the Townsends were coming.

Charlie had been near the office the previous afternoon, and he told Samantha that he'd overheard Brad phoning Johnston to tell him that he and his father would come over to inspect the barn at five.

"I guess all we can do," Ashleigh told Samantha when Samantha called her, "is keep an eye on Johnston ourselves. I don't think Brad will bother, and I'm not going to let him neglect Wonder."

"Well, Petie and Micky said they'd check up on her from time to time," Samantha said.

"But we both know how overworked they are."

Over the next couple of weeks, Johnston kept the breeding barns somewhat cleaner, but he definitely didn't exert himself. Samantha went down to check on Wonder every day, rain or shine, and Ashleigh did too, whenever she could. Johnston was curt and unfriendly as always toward Samantha, but more often than not, he wasn't around.

Nothing seemed to be going well around the farm. The staff was no longer relaxed or as quick to laugh and stop for a chat. And Hank, who had been at the farm longer than any of the other staff, frequently commented on the lagging morale. Samantha tried to cheer herself up with the thought that Pride would soon go back in training, but she couldn't ignore the tension that hung in the air.

The cold spell broke in late January, and the weather turned unseasonably warm for several days. On the last day of the month, Samantha returned home from school, quickly changed into her work clothes, then went straight out to Pride's stall to give him his daily grooming.

Samantha laughed when she saw him. "Just look at you!" she said. "What a mess!"

Hank had put Pride out in the paddock for some exercise along with the other horses who had just turned two years old, and the colt had obviously wasted no time in taking a luxurious roll on the muddy turf. He thrust his noble nose into the air, then ambled across his stall to nudge Samantha.

"Yeah, I know," Samantha said. "You had a ball. Well, let's start cleaning some of that mud off." She took a currycomb and started to work on the

89

crusted dirt while Pride craned his neck around and watched her. He didn't seem the least bit upset that he was causing her so much work.

She had progressed to a dandy brush when she heard footsteps outside the stall.

"Sammy—" she heard Ashleigh say from just outside the stall.

Samantha turned around with a smile on her lips—but then she saw Ashleigh's white face. "What's wrong?" Samantha cried. "You look terrible!"

"I feel terrible," Ashleigh said with effort. She gripped the top of the stall door with white-knuckled hands. "I've just come from Mr. Townsend's office. He thinks he's going to have to sell his half-interest in Wonder . . . and maybe Wonder's Pride!"

Samantha gasped. "No!"

"I . . . I don't want to believe it either," Ashleigh said. "He says he's had some very bad financial news."

Samantha's head reeled. "How can he sell Wonder?" she cried. "She's a champion. She's the best mare on the farm!"

"She also hasn't had a foal in two years."

"But—but—"

"He doesn't want to sell her," Ashleigh explained in stunned tones. "It's just that he may have to raise a lot of money fast . . . and Wonder is worth the most."

"What about the stallions?"

"He'd never sell his good stallions," Ashleigh explained. "Without the stallions, they'd never have a chance of breeding any outstanding horses. The farm makes so much in stud fees, and they've already lost Prince."

"And they might sell their interest in Pride, too?"

Ashleigh nodded weakly.

"But he's the best two-year-old they have!"

"And he's worth the most money. Someone has already approached Mr. Townsend, asking if Pride might be for sale."

Samantha couldn't believe what she was hearing. "But you still own a half-interest."

Ashleigh nodded. "That's why he came to me first—to see if I wanted to buy the Townsend interest. But I can't raise that much money. All Wonder's earnings are in a trust fund, and Goddess's earnings aren't enough after I figure for all the expenses."

"How much money would you need?"

"Around a million."

Samantha's mouth dropped open. "A million dollars?"

"It could go even higher," Ashleigh said. "Wonder's the most valuable broodmare on the East Coast, and an interest in Pride would bring big bucks. He hasn't proven himself at the track yet, but with his bloodlines, he'll be worth a lot at stud."

91

Samantha walked over to Pride and laid a hand on his shoulder. She felt dizzy and sick. "What are you going to do?"

Ashleigh shook her head. "I don't know . . . I just don't know. I need to talk to my parents, and maybe Mike could chip in some money—but I don't think he has much extra."

"There must be other horses they could sell," Samantha said desperately.

"Haven't you noticed how much of the stock has already gone to auction?"

"Brad's two colts," Samantha said angrily. "Why don't they sell them?"

"Neither of them has lifted a hoof. The Townsends would *never* get back what Brad paid for them." Ashleigh leaned both her elbows on the stall door and shook her head miserably. After a few moments she said, "All I can hope is that Mr. Townsend will find another way to raise money."

"If he does sell his interest," Samantha asked weakly, "what will happen to Wonder and Pride? Will they stay here?"

"There'd be no reason for them to stay here. Wonder could go to my parents' place, but the new half-owner will have something to say about it. They might not agree with me about where Wonder should go, or agree on Pride's training schedule. If they're paying that kind of money, they probably won't want to leave the training to me. They might want a top trainer taking over."

"Charlie's a top trainer," Samantha reminded her.

"Yeah, but he works for Townsend Acres. It could be a real mess. Mr. Townsend has given me and Charlie pretty much a free hand. A new owner might have different ideas."

Samantha saw clearly that she'd have no part in Pride's training at all if new owners bought in. Pride and Wonder would be leaving the farm, and she wouldn't be able to work with him anymore. She felt a rush of anger. How could the Townsends' problems have such a horrible effect on so many people?

"I'm sorry, Sammy," Ashleigh said quietly. "I know how you feel about Wonder and Pride."

"We've got to do something!" Samantha cried.

"I haven't given up yet," Ashleigh said with determination. "I'll talk to Mr. Townsend again and see if I can convince him to change his mind. I've got to go meet Mike now. Maybe he'll have some ideas."

"Call me and let me know," Samantha said desperately.

"I'll call you tonight," Ashleigh promised.

Samantha was barely aware of what she was doing as she finished Pride's grooming. It was too much to absorb. She didn't want to believe it. "They can't sell you," she whispered to the horse. "I don't know how I'll be able to stand it if they take you away from the farm!"

The colt gently nudged her with his nose, as if he sensed some of her misery. Samantha laid her cheek against his neck. As she did, she saw Charlie approaching the stall.

"Looks like you've heard," Charlie said.

Samantha nodded mutely. "Ashleigh just told me. She's gone to talk to Mike."

"Just talked to her myself." The old trainer pushed back his hat and scowled. "So it's come to that—selling some of the best stock on the farm!"

Samantha could see that Charlie was upset, more so than she'd ever seen him.

"That filly ran her heart out for this farm," Charlie muttered angrily. "Earned them huge purses and added to their reputation. Now they're willing to sell her and her colt. Doesn't seem right! I can't believe Townsend would do it."

"From what Ashleigh said, they're desperate for money."

"Hmph. They might not be in these straits if it weren't for some poor judgments made around here." His mouth tightened. "I don't suppose Ashleigh can get her hands on the money to buy him out."

Samantha shook her head. "She doesn't think so."

"Well, there's still a chance Townsend will come to his senses." The old trainer stomped off, probably to talk to Hank. In a daze, Samantha stowed Pride's grooming brushes, gave the colt a last hug, and went back to the apartment. As soon as she was inside, she went to the phone and called Yvonne.

"It can't be as bad as that," Yvonne said. "I mean, the Townsends are rich—really rich. Look at that huge house they have on the farm."

"Yeah, I guess," Samantha said glumly.

"It will get better," Yvonne said in a comforting tone, but Samantha wasn't reassured. She hung up the phone and sat down at the kitchen table. It was time to start dinner, but food was the last thing she wanted to think about. She buried her face in her hands. The situation at Townsend Acres was more serious than she had ever imagined.

When her father came in a few minutes later, she saw from the expression on his face that she was right.

He took one look at her and sighed. "I see you know," he said, sitting down beside her. "Everyone's talking about it. I'm sorry, sweetheart. It's got to be a blow to you. How's Ashleigh?"

Samantha told him about the conversation she'd had with Ashleigh that afternoon.

"It's such a foolish move," her father said tiredly. "Maddock and I were talking, and we both think it's nuts to sell out their interest in the one horse that could turn the farm's racing fortunes around again. We both see the potential in Pride. And Wonder is bound to have another foal. From what I hear, she checks out with a clean bill of health." He ran his fingers through his hair. "Townsend might still change his mind. I think he may have reacted in panic. I've always respected his decisions in the past, except that he's given that kid of his too much responsibility too fast. We'll see." He reached over and took his daughter's hand and gave her a weak smile. "Come on, let's get out of here for a while. We'll go into town and splurge on a good dinner."

Samantha nodded. She certainly didn't want to hang around the apartment, with nothing but miserable thoughts on her mind.

The next day in school, Samantha could barely concentrate. Her math teacher gave her a surprised look when she fumbled over a question she would normally have answered easily and correctly. In the halls between classes, she was oblivious to the smiles and waves of other kids, and at lunch, Yvonne kept throwing worried glances her way. After lunch, when she was at her locker, she felt a gentle tap on her shoulder. She turned to see Tor Nelson standing behind her.

"What's wrong?" he asked. "You walked right past me just now, as if you didn't see me."

Samantha tried to pull herself together. "I'm sorry. I've just got a lot on my mind."

Tor looked at her with concern, and she explained what had happened.

"There isn't anything you can do?" he asked.

"I can't do anything," Samantha answered. "But maybe Ashleigh can. I don't know. When she called me last night, she said she didn't have any solutions yet. We're going to talk to Mr. Townsend this afternoon. Though I don't know if it'll do any good."

"I'll keep my fingers crossed for you," Tor said. "I know what a mess I'd be if I thought I might lose Top Hat."

Samantha was a wreck. Could she and Ashleigh persuade Mr. Townsend to change his mind? Horses like Wonder and Wonder's Pride didn't come along every day—sometimes not in a lifetime.

Ashleigh looked as apprehensive as Samantha felt when she drove up to Townsend Acres later that day. "Keep hoping," she said as the two girls headed toward Mr. Townsend's office.

Mr. Townsend motioned them in when he saw them outside his office. He'd been expecting them to stop in. They sat down in the two chairs facing his paper-strewn desk, and Samantha's eyes immediately focused on a framed picture hanging on the wall. It was a color photo of Wonder after she'd won the Kentucky Derby. Jilly sat proudly in the mare's saddle, and Ashleigh was standing at the filly's head, beaming. Things sure had changed.

"I can't raise the money to buy out your interest, Mr. Townsend," Ashleigh said. "Most of what I have is in a trust fund, and I can't touch it until I'm twenty-one, except for my college expenses. I have some cash from Goddess's winnings, but it's not nearly enough."

Clay Townsend rested his arms on his desk. He looked tired and drawn. "I was afraid of that." He sighed heavily. "But I wanted you to have the first opportunity."

Ashleigh leaned forward in her chair. "Mr. Townsend, can't we persuade you to change your mind about selling? Isn't there some other way for you to raise money? Wonder is just too special to the farm. I know I'll still have my interest in her, but I don't know what another half-owner will do. And Pride is coming along so well. He has incredible potential."

"He could be a great racehorse, Mr. Townsend," Samantha put in. "He's eager and quick to learn, and he has beautiful movements. Charlie, my father, and Mr. Maddock all think he's the best horse coming into training."

"I don't doubt any of that," Townsend said. "You know I've always had high hopes for the colt. But the fact that he is showing talent makes him all the more valuable."

"But he's too good to sell," Samantha pleaded. "When he starts racing, he'll make money for the farm."

Mr. Townsend gave her a sad smile. "The problem is that I don't know if we can wait that long. Look, I don't want to sell my interest in either of them, but I don't have many options."

"Are you thinking of selling Wonder because she hasn't had a foal in two years?" Ashleigh asked.

"That's a consideration, but it's not the only reason. In fact, I was going to suggest that we go ahead and breed her again next week to Baldasar. He's one of our best stallions."

Ashleigh nodded. "Yes, I was hoping you would."

"But even if she gets in foal this time," Townsend added, "I don't know if it will change my decision."

"Can't you just think about it a little longer, Mr. Townsend?" Ashleigh pleaded. "It's only another week before Pride goes back into training. He could be racing by June."

He sighed again, and Samantha could see he was torn. "Let me think about it, Ashleigh. But let me warn you—someone may be coming over to look at Pride in the next couple of weeks."

Samantha felt her stomach sink to her feet.

"I won't formalize any sale without discussing it with you first, but the interested party is very respected in the industry."

Ashleigh nodded, then rose slowly from her seat. "I really hope things will work out, so you won't have to sell."

"Believe me, I hope so too," Mr. Townsend said. "But I'm just not in a position to make any promises."

After the girls had left his office, Samantha said softly, "It doesn't sound very good, does it?"

Ashleigh pursed her lips and shook her head. "No. I know he doesn't want to sell, but he's made it pretty clear that things are bad."

"What do we do now?" Samantha asked.

"I guess we just try to go on as if everything were normal. Start Pride's training next week and hope Wonder gets in foal."

"It's not going to be easy."

"No," Ashleigh said. "It's not."

8

NOTHING HAPPENED IN THE NEXT WEEK TO CHEER Samantha up. Mr. Townsend hadn't changed his mind about the possibility of selling Wonder and Pride, and he'd left on another business trip. The general mood on the farm was getting worse and worse, and Brad seemed to be the only one who wasn't affected by the heavy atmosphere. He acted like nothing was wrong, buzzing in and out in his Ferarri and irritating the staff with his bossiness.

Fortunately training started up again, and Samantha had much more to do to keep her mind off her fears. First, she and Charlie started working Pride on the longe line, preparing him for the more hectic training schedule ahead, and then Samantha started riding him at a walk, trot, and

101

canter on the straight galloping lane beyond the stables.

"The last couple of days have gone really well," she told Yvonne at lunch one day. "Pride hasn't forgotten a thing from his fall training."

"I just hope the Townsends suddenly find a bundle of money," Yvonne said. "Nobody's come to look at him yet?"

"No," Samantha answered, crushing her sandwich wrapper, "but Mr. Townsend said someone would. It scares me."

"Well, even if this buyer is really impressed, it doesn't mean Townsend will sell," Yvonne argued.

Samantha looked across at her friend and shook her head. "I wish I could be as optimistic as you."

"Well, worrying only makes you feel crummier," Yvonne said. "At least that's what my mother tells me. Listen, why don't you come to the basketball game with me on Friday afternoon? It would take your mind off things."

"Actually, Tor's already asked me."

"Aha!" Yvonne said, grinning. "Keeping secrets from me!"

Samantha smiled at her friend's reaction. "He mentioned it only this morning when I saw him between classes."

"So he finally asked you for a date."

"It's *not* a date," Samantha said. "Tor and I

102

are just friends. Besides, why would he ask someone two years younger than he is out on a date?"

"So what if he's a little older?" Yvonne said. "You guys get along really well."

Samantha rolled her eyes, choosing to ignore Yvonne's comments. "The game's right after school," she said. "We're just going over to the gym together. And he said he'd give me a ride home so that I can show him Pride."

Yvonne's grin widened.

"You're too much," Samantha told her.

"Are you guys talking horses again?" Maureen O'Brian, a pixie of a brunette, walked up to them. She and Samantha sat next to each other in homeroom and had become friends.

"You have something against horses?" Yvonne said.

"You know I like horses," Maureen protested. "I'm just not into them like you two are. Of course, I don't live on a training farm either, like Sammy does. Anyway, I'm trying to get some new columns started for the school newspaper, and I had this idea." She looked at Samantha. "I thought, well, here we are living right in the middle of racing country, and there's nothing in the school newspaper about it. So Sammy, I was wondering if you'd like to write a monthly column for us—you know, about what the big farms are doing, what goes on at the track—that kind of stuff. You know all about it, and it doesn't have to be long."

Samantha looked at Maureen with interest. "Sure, why not?" she said after a moment. "That would be fun."

"You'll do it!" Maureen exclaimed. "Wow, that's great! I didn't think you would."

"Why not?" Samantha asked.

"Because you're so busy with training and everything." Maureen started flipping through her notebook. "Let's see, the deadline for the March issue is late next week. Is that too soon?"

"No, I could get something written. How long does it have to be?"

"Two notebook pages should be enough," Maureen said.

Samantha grinned. "I might have trouble keeping it that short."

"Three pages, then," Maureen said excitedly. "Maybe I can get them to run it as a feature." She frowned. "Well, we'll see. Being a lousy little freshman, I don't always get much say. So you can get it to me by the end of next week?"

"Sure," Samantha said. "This is great. You know, I was thinking of joining the newspaper staff. Does this make me a member?"

"It should," Maureen said. "Though you'll have to come to some meetings, too. They're every Thursday after school."

"Okay. I'll be at the next meeting."

"All right!" Maureen said, beaming. "Half my

job is done. Now, Yvonne, I know you're part Navajo. How'd you like to write a little piece about Navajo customs . . ."

Yvonne was laughing before the words were out of Maureen's mouth. "Now, why did I think that was coming?" she said. "Sure, but someone's going to have to check my spelling and stuff. English isn't my favorite subject."

"No prob," Maureen said.

Later, when Samantha had taken her seat in study hall, she smiled to herself. The more she thought about it, the more she liked the idea of writing a monthly column. She would certainly never run out of things to say about Thoroughbreds and racing. Flipping open her notebook, she started jotting some notes. She could start the article that night after she finished her homework.

On the first Friday in February, Pride was ready to go out to the track for more intensive training. Samantha led him eagerly from the barn toward the mist-enveloped oval, where Ashleigh and Charlie waited in the chill morning air. Johnny Byard would be riding too, on one of the other two-year-olds who had trained with Pride in the fall. Two of the other horses at Pride's stage of training had been sold at the Keeneland auction the previous month. Samantha had heard that they hadn't brought what the Townsends had hoped.

Maybe if they had, the Townsends wouldn't be forced into selling their interest in Wonder and Pride.

Samantha scowled, then pushed the unpleasant thought out of her mind. This was too important a morning to let unhappy thoughts intrude. But then she saw Brad farther up the rail with his two expensive plodders, now three-year-olds. Even at a distance, Samantha could see the expressions on her father's and Maddock's faces, and it was obvious that Brad was giving them trouble about something.

"We'll show Brad what a good horse looks like," she said to Pride. "Yeah, you're excited, aren't you? You remember this place." The colt had his head up and ears pricked and was toe-dancing at the end of his lead. "From now on, you'll be out there nearly every morning. Hi, Ash. Hi, Charlie," she called as she led Pride toward them.

"Mornin'," Charlie said, eyeing the colt.

"Charlie and I were just talking about Pride's schedule," Ashleigh said to Samantha. "We thought it would be good to start him on some long, slow gallops, at least for the next couple of days. Then gradually we'll work him up to short breezes."

Samantha nodded.

"There's going to be a lot to do in the next couple of months," Ashleigh went on, but as she spoke, a cloud passed over her features. "If we *have* a couple of months to work him. Anyway, we'll need to teach him to break, first from a standing start, then from the gate. By that time we should have figured out how he likes to run—on or off the pace—"

"Getting a bit ahead of yourself, aren't you?" Charlie put in. "Haven't even gotten him out on the track again."

"I know," Ashleigh said, "but I've been thinking about it for so long."

"Up you go, missy," Charlie said to Samantha, giving her a leg into Pride's saddle. "Work with Johnny for today, till these young colts settle into the routine again. Maddock has the same game plan as we do. After they're warmed up, you can let them out into a slow gallop. The colt might pressure you for more after being cooped up for most of the winter, but don't let him have his head. He'll need to build his muscles up little by little."

Samantha nodded. She knew what to do, and she also knew that working a young horse too fast too soon did more harm than good.

Although the February morning air was crisp, the ground wasn't frozen, and the harrows run over the track had dried the worst of the mud. She urged Pride toward the gap to meet Johnny, and moments later the two of them set off at a trot up the track.

Pride was bubbling with high spirits, but

Samantha kept him firmly in hand, and because he trusted her, the colt obeyed. She felt him tug at the reins a few times, testing her, but he settled down to business as soon as they increased speed to a canter. Eventually both riders set their mounts to a slow gallop.

As Samantha crouched over Pride's withers, she was amazed at the smoothness and power of his stride. He did it all so effortlessly, as if he were taking an amble in the park, rather than a gallop on the oval. He had so much talent! Samantha thought. And she might not be able to see it develop. Yet for a few short minutes as they pounded around the track, she could forget about the possibility of losing him and simply enjoy herself.

"He hasn't lost any of his spark," Johnny said with a wink as they rode off the track after the workout. "Too bad certain owners don't wake up."

"They know how good he is."

"Maybe the old man does," Johnny answered, "but the kid is sure behind the sale from what I hear."

Samantha threw him a questioning look.

Johnny shrugged. "Just talk. He can't stand to see the best colt on the farm in Ashleigh's and Charlie's hands. Rather cut off his nose to spite his face."

Samantha could certainly believe that about

Brad. But it was Mr. Townsend who would make the decision, not Brad, and in her heart she knew Mr. Townsend didn't want to sell.

Pride received all the admiring comments he deserved as Samantha rode over to the trainers and other riders and dismounted.

"If he keeps up like that," she heard Maddock say to Charlie, "you'll have something. Nice temperament, too. Didn't see him fighting her at all, which isn't always the case with a green horse."

"Sammy's got a way with him," Charlie admitted gruffly. "Kid's got nice gentle hands and a good seat."

Charlie's back was facing her, and Samantha knew he hadn't intended her to overhear the compliment, but she flushed with pleasure as she reached up to rub Pride's neck. *Charlie thinks I'm a good rider*, she thought. *And he'd never say it if he didn't mean it!*

Since Samantha would be riding Goddess next, she turned Pride over to Hank, who led the colt off to the stable. Ashleigh only wanted to give Goddess a light work, but as usual the filly put in a shining performance.

When they came off the track, Ashleigh held the filly's head so Samantha could dismount. "I'm feeling good about her four-year-old season," Ashleigh said. "She's right on her toes. Good ride, Sammy."

"Thanks, but she makes it easy."

As the two girls led Goddess back to the barn, Samantha repeated what Johnny had told her about Brad.

"Pretty much what I thought," Ashleigh said. "I'll bet Brad thinks that if they sell out their interest in Wonder and Pride, he can go out and buy himself another horse."

"Which will probably be just as much a dud as the others," Samantha added drily.

Ashleigh laughed, then quickly sobered. "But it's not anything to laugh about, is it?"

"No," Samantha agreed.

After school that day, Tor met Samantha at her locker. Together they walked over and watched the basketball game, which turned out to be a disappointment because Henry Clay lost. But neither of them were basketball fans, and as Tor drove to Townsend Acres, they naturally started talking about horses.

"I guess you haven't heard anything more about Pride being sold," he said.

"No, and sometimes I think not knowing is harder than knowing the worst. Though I don't know what I'm going to do if Pride leaves the farm."

"There aren't any other horses you could concentrate on?"

"Nothing special, though I suppose there could

always be a surprise. But Pride isn't just *any* horse. I've been around him since he was foaled, taken care of him . . . helped train him . . . and I know he's going to be incredible."

They reached Townsend Acres and drove up the long, tree-lined drive, past the breeding barns, to the parking lot by the training area. Samantha spotted Brad's Ferrari parked near the office and hoped they didn't bump into him.

"This place is huge," Tor said admiringly.

"It is," Samantha agreed as they got out of Tor's car. "This is the training area. All the horses stabled here are active racing stock. Over there"—she motioned across the stable yard—"is the training oval. It's a full-mile track. A lot of training centers only have half- or three-quarter-mile tracks. There's a turf galloping lane up beyond the stable buildings, and all kinds of trails. Then there's the breeding area, which we passed on the way up the drive. All the broodmares and stallions are kept there—in separate quarters. The young horses stay in the breeding area until they're yearlings. Then they're moved to the yearling barns and paddocks up here in the training area."

"You know a lot about the operation," Tor said.

"You can't help it when you live here," Samantha explained. "And Ashleigh's parents used to be the breeding managers, so she's told me a lot about that. I go down nearly every day to visit her mare, Wonder. Have you heard of her?"

111

"The filly who won the Kentucky Derby?" Tor said, smiling. "Everyone remembers Derby winners."

"Yeah. She's pretty special. But come on, let me show you Pride, her first foal." Samantha led the way toward the stable building where Pride was stalled. "I think you'll like him."

She opened the door at the end of the building and Tor followed her in. "This barn has about twenty stalls. The other two barns have about the same. You can see that half of the stalls are empty now, they've sold off so much stock. Only about thirty horses are left in active training. Pride's down here just around the corner." Samantha led the way, walking slowly so that Tor could have a look at the horses they passed. She heard voices at the other end of the building, but that wasn't surprising. There would be grooms at work, cleaning tack and tending to other chores.

But as she rounded the corner, she stopped dead in her tracks. Brad had taken Pride out of his stall, and a stranger was inspecting the colt. Pride skittered at the end of his lead and looked confused by the change in his usual routine. Brad jiggled the lead to get the colt's attention. "You can see he's got his dam's conformation," Brad said to the stranger. "He's been training beautifully."

"So I've heard," the stranger said, "but I'd like to see him work before I make any firm commitments." He was an older man with thick, iron-gray hair that was neatly combed. His tailored topcoat looked expensive, and when he raised a hand to run it down Pride's back, Samantha saw the flash of a gold ring. Whoever he was, everything about him said power and money.

He had to be the interested buyer Mr. Townsend mentioned, Samantha thought. Seeing the man's genuine admiration for the colt and knowing he could be the colt's new half-owner made Samantha feel sick.

Tor touched her arm and mouthed the word "Pride?"

Samantha nodded. She didn't know what to do. She was furious, but Brad had every right to show Pride to the stranger. She couldn't try to stop him.

It was Pride who first noticed her and Tor standing at the turn of the aisle. As Brad walked the colt in a small circle, continuing to show him off to the stranger, Pride looked in Samantha's direction, flared his delicate nostrils, and gave a happy whinny of greeting. He stopped in his tracks and bobbed his head, waiting for Samantha to come to him.

Both men turned to stare at Samantha and Tor. Brad's eyes flicked over Tor, but focused on Samantha. "We're busy right now, Sammy. You can come back and groom him later," he said shortly. Then he turned his back on her dismissively.

But Pride wasn't about to ignore Samantha, and he strained against the lead, trying to walk in her direction. When Brad held firm, he tossed his head angrily, pranced on his hindquarters, and then whinnied to Samantha again.

The stranger was studying the colt's behavior with a thoughtful frown. "You're his groom?" he said to her.

"Yes," she answered with a tight throat.

"He seems to have formed a bond with you. You might as well come over and say hello to him. I don't think he's going to settle down otherwise."

Feeling wooden, Samantha went over and took Pride's head in her hands. "Yeah, boy," she soothed, "I'm glad to see you, too. I'll be back later to feed you and give you a good brushing." In answer, the colt blew softly against her cheek. "I've got to go now," she added in a near whisper.

The stranger turned to Brad. "I can't stay to watch tomorrow morning's workouts," he said. "I have to get back to New York. I'll arrange to come back down sometime next week."

"Fine," Brad said smoothly. "Whatever you like. You'll stay at the house, of course. My father would want you to . . ."

Before she could hear any more, Samantha hurried back to Tor. It sounded very much like Mr. Townsend had made his decision. He was going to sell. Samantha wanted to scream. She wanted to cry. She didn't want to do either in front of Tor, but her emotions must have shown on her face.

He seemed embarrassed that he'd been there. "Not very good timing for my visit, I guess."

"I can't believe it," Samantha said, tightening her hands into balls. "Mr. Townsend hasn't said a word to Ashleigh about deciding to sell."

"Maybe he hasn't," Tor said. "Didn't you tell me that someone had approached him about selling his interest in the colt?"

"Yes. He said someone would be coming by. But that man sounded so definite—like Mr. Townsend had agreed."

"I don't know. He's a businessman. He's supposed to sound strong, especially if he wants to persuade Townsend to sell."

Samantha tried to think clearly, but it was almost impossible. She was boiling inside, and she wanted to talk to Ashleigh.

"Look," Tor said gently. "This isn't a good time for you. You probably want to be by yourself. I'd better get going."

Samantha sighed and nodded.

"I'll see you on Monday," he said. "This afternoon was great, and really, don't think the worst yet."

Samantha gave him a wobbly smile. "Thanks, Tor. I had a good time too. I'm sorry about all of this. I'm sorry I'm such a mess over it."

"Hey, listen, it's not your fault. Just hang in there."

"I will. I'll see you in school on Monday."

As soon as he drove off, Samantha rushed to the apartment. She slammed the door behind her to get rid of some of her anger, then raced for the phone to call Ashleigh.

9

ASHLEIGH CALLED SAMANTHA THE NEXT MORNING AS
soon as she'd gotten in touch with Mr. Townsend
in New York. "Mr. Townsend hasn't made a decision yet," Ashleigh said. "He said he's trying to
work out another financial arrangement so he
doesn't have to sell his interest."

Samantha felt weak-kneed with relief. She'd
been so frightened, she hadn't been able to keep
her mind on anything.

"But it bothers me that that buyer seemed so interested. His name is Myron Yeakel. Have you
heard of him?"

"He owns a big farm in New York State, doesn't
he?"

"And smaller ones in Kentucky and Florida."

"Oh." Samantha frowned. "He *is* big time."

117

"Very," Ashleigh answered. "And if he does buy out a half-interest in Pride, I think I'm going to have trouble. He's not going to want to listen to me."

"But Mr. Townsend's really trying to work something out so he can keep Wonder and Pride?" Samantha asked anxiously.

"That's what he said on the phone, though he still wouldn't make any promises."

"At least it's something," Samantha said.

"Yes." Ashleigh sighed. "Oh, and did you know Wonder was bred yesterday?"

"She was?"

"Yeah, and Johnston and Tom say everything went all right. Tom would know, since he's the stallion manager."

"And I didn't even get a chance to go down to see her yesterday, I was so upset about Pride," Samantha said regretfully.

"Well, how did things look at the breeding barns the last time you were there?"

"Okay, I guess. But they're still shorthanded, and Petie told me that Johnston is doing less and less of the work. He's only around when he thinks someone might come visiting."

"If I find he's neglecting Wonder, I'll go straight to Mr. Townsend," Ashleigh said firmly.

Samantha concentrated all her energy on Pride's training for the rest of the month, working

118

him every morning when the weather was decent. She tried not to think of Myron Yeakel or the fact that Mr. Townsend still hadn't made any firm decisions. Yeakel had come with Brad and Mr. Townsend the week before to watch Pride's workout. Afterward, he'd seemed pleased with what he'd seen, and approached Charlie to ask about the colt's training schedule.

They talked about Pride's progress for a few minutes with Ashleigh within hearing distance, then Charlie asked, "You met the colt's other owner yet?"

Yeakel had given Ashleigh a startled look. It was obvious that he hadn't expected Pride's other owner to be so young. Then he'd smiled almost condescendingly and nodded at her. He didn't offer to shake her hand, and only turned to study the colt once more before walking back to the Townsends.

His attitude had bothered Samantha. How dare he treat Ashleigh like that, she'd thought.

Ashleigh had seemed disturbed by his coldness toward her too. "I knew he'd be trouble," she'd said angrily after Yeakel left.

A week later, Mr. Townsend turned up at the oval for the morning workouts, and for the first time in a long while, he was smiling. He walked over to Ashleigh and Samantha.

"Well, I just heard from the vet," he said. "The preliminary tests seem to indicate that Wonder is definitely in foal."

"Fantastic!" both girls said.

His smile widened. "Now we'll just have to keep our fingers crossed that all goes well."

That Friday, Yvonne came over after school to spend the night. After they had changed into jeans and T-shirts and had a snack, they headed out into the sunny March day. There was the feel of spring in the air, and everyone seemed to be in lighter spirits—even the horses. It was a welcome relief from the gloomy atmosphere that had been around all winter.

"I want to check on Wonder," Samantha said, shining an apple on her sleeve. "One of the breeding grooms is sick, and I don't trust Johnston to do the extra work."

The girls started down the drive. "This place is really gorgeous," Yvonne said, looking out over the pastures.

"It is," Samantha agreed. *And it was once a happy place too*, she added in her thoughts.

When they entered the mares' barn, Samantha's face paled. The barn was a mess! The aisle was filthy and hadn't been swept or hosed, and no one was in sight. Samantha and Yvonne went from stall to stall, gasping at what they saw. Not one of them had been mucked out, and some hay nets and water buckets were empty!

Samantha was also surprised to find that all the mares were in their stalls. At least a few of them should have been let out into the paddock on such a beautiful day. Two of the mares had foaled in the past week, and many others were close to foaling.

Wonder whinnied loudly, deliriously happy to see them as they reached her stall.

"Oh, girl!" Samantha cried, opening the stall door. "What are they doing to you? You poor thing!" Samantha hugged the mare's neck. Her beautiful copper coat was marred by dirt and bedding. It was clear that no grooming brush had touched her that day, and the stall bedding needed to be changed. Samantha glanced into Wonder's water bucket. Bone dry. And her hay net was empty.

"Oh, my gosh!" Yvonne said in shock. "This is awful!"

Without thinking, Samantha grabbed Wonder's lead shank from outside the stall and clipped it to the mare's halter. "You aren't staying in here another second, girl!"

Wonder nudged her and whinnied low in her throat.

But when Samantha started leading Wonder out into the aisle, Johnston suddenly loomed out of the darkness at the back of the barn near the feed and storage rooms.

"What do you think you're doing?" he shouted.

"I'm taking her out of this pigsty!" Samantha shouted back. "These mares don't have food or water. Their stalls are filthy. It's disgusting!"

Johnston moved quickly toward her. "You're not taking her anywhere. These mares are in my charge," he growled.

Samantha cringed from the scent of alcohol on his breath. "You don't deserve to be in charge. Look at this place!"

"Get out!" he told her ominously. "Leave that mare right where she is and get out!"

"I'm not going anywhere unless she comes with me!" Samantha was too angry to be afraid, but she knew she didn't stand a chance against Johnston, who outweighed her by at least a hundred pounds.

He came into the stall and grabbed the lead shank out of her hand, then he shoved her out into the aisle. "Now get out! I've had all I'm going to take of you, you meddling brat!"

Wonder whinnied again loudly, but this time in fear. She threw up her head and tried to lunge forward out of the stall. Johnston backhanded her and caught her on the nose. "Get back there, you!"

Wonder screeched in pain.

Samantha was horrified. She needed help. "Let's go," she called to Yvonne, who was staring at Johnston wide-eyed. "I'll be back, Wonder!"

The two girls raced down the barn aisle. "Stay here and watch through the crack in the door. See what he does," Samantha told Yvonne when they were outside. "I've got to get help."

Yvonne looked frightened, but she nodded. Samantha tore up the drive and rushed across the stable yard, yelling at the top of her lungs. "Dad! Charlie! Hank! Help!"

Staff members appeared from all sides almost immediately. "What's going on?" someone asked.

"Where's my father? Where's Charlie?" Samantha said breathlessly. Just then her father and Charlie hurried out from the barns, along with Hank and Mr. Maddock.

"What's wrong?" Mr. McLean cried.

"It's Johnston. He's been drinking. The mares don't have feed or water. He started pushing me around when I tried to take Wonder—"

"Good God," her father said. "Someone go get Townsend and send him down to the mares' barn!"

"I'll get him," Charlie said.

Mr. McLean quickly turned and started jogging down the drive. Samantha ran beside him, with Hank and Maddock hurrying behind.

Yvonne called to them when they reached the barn. "He left Wonder in her stall and went to the back of the barn," she reported. "He hasn't come out again."

Samantha and the men swung open the barn door. Anxious whinnies came out of almost every stall. Samantha went straight to Wonder, who still looked frightened. "It's okay, girl. I'm back. You won't have to put up with him anymore. That's it, easy, girl," she said as she stroked the mare's neck.

123

Behind her, Samantha heard the men's exclamations of horror. "I don't believe this!" Maddock cried. "How could anyone leave these animals in this state?"

"I'm going to find Johnston!" her father said furiously.

"I'll start filling some of these water buckets," Hank offered. "You poor ladies," he added to the whickering mares. "And darn, if there aren't a couple of foals in here, too. Guy ought to be shot."

Clay Townsend and Charlie hurried into the barn just as Samantha's father was hauling a staggering Johnston up the aisle from the storeroom. Johnston focused his bleary eyes on Samantha and made an ugly face. "You! I told you to get out of here!"

He was so drunk, he didn't seem to realize his predicament. Mr. Townsend was striding up and down the aisle, looking into stalls, his expression growing blacker and blacker.

"I want you off my property by nightfall!" he boomed.

"Not my fault," the breeding manager whined. "I'm shorthanded. A groom's sick."

"Shorthanded and falling down drunk!" Mr. Townsend roared. "There are no excuses for this kind of neglect—and no excuses for your behavior to Samantha. Get your belongings and get out of here! Ken and Ian, take him over to his house and see that he starts packing."

"With pleasure," Mr. McLean said, grabbing hold of Johnston's arm. Maddock strode over to take his other arm, a look of disgust on his face. By now the breeding manager realized he didn't have a chance to save himself, but he *did* have enough energy to sneer to Samantha, "It's all your fault, little sneak."

Then he suddenly yelped, "My arm!"

"Right," Mr. McLean said, "and I'll give it another twist if you don't shut your mouth. That's my daughter you're talking to—and frankly, I'm proud of her!"

Johnston shut up, and Mr. McLean and Maddock dragged him out of the barn. Before they were out of sight, Mr. Townsend went to the phone in Johnston's office and called the training area. "Send down all the extra grooms you can spare, and is my son back yet? All right, when he gets back, tell him to wait for me in my office."

Samantha was already unhooking Wonder's water bucket and heading toward one of the taps along the aisle. Hank and Charlie were busy on the other side of the aisle, and Yvonne was helping them. Petie, one of the regular breeding grooms, hurried into the barn and stared about wide-eyed. "What's going on?" he asked in amazement. "Why is everyone here?"

Mr. Townsend explained the situation.

Petie shook his head sadly. "I just finished up in the foaling barn. . . . I've been working alone. I've

125

been doing the best I can, but Johnston hasn't lifted a finger."

"We know you're not responsible for this," Townsend said. "I've sacked Johnston. If you're not too tired, maybe you could give Hank and Charlie a hand."

"Sure," Petie said.

Two grooms from the training area arrived, and Hank and Charlie set them to work immediately. Soon they were leading mares out so the stalls could be cleaned. The two-week-old foals wobbled out of their stalls, pressing themselves to their mothers' sides.

Mr. Townsend came up to Samantha as she was filling Wonder's bucket with cool, fresh water. "You and Ashleigh were right about Johnston," he said. "I can't believe this was going on right under my nose."

"It wasn't always this bad," Samantha admitted. "Today was the worst I've ever seen it, but Johnston definitely wasn't doing his job properly."

"Well, he'll be gone soon, and I'll make sure his replacement does the job right!"

Then Ashleigh came running into the barn. She stopped in her tracks and stared all around her before hurrying down the aisle toward Samantha and Mr. Townsend. "They told me up at the training area what happened," she said breathlessly. "How's Wonder?"

"A little nervous, but she's okay. I'm bringing her water," Samantha said, hoisting the pail.

Ashleigh went to Wonder's stall and let herself in. She hugged the mare's neck, then took the pail from Samantha and set it in front of the thirsty horse. Wonder whickered her appreciation as she dipped her mouth in the bucket.

"How long were the mares without feed and water?" Ashleigh asked.

"I don't know," Samantha said. "Yvonne and I came down right after we got home from school. It didn't look like anyone had touched the barn all day. Micky is sick, and Petie was working in the foaling barn."

"We'll start looking for another breeding manager immediately," Mr. Townsend told Ashleigh. "And in the meantime, I'll have a couple of the training grooms pitch in and help around here. It'll mean extra work for everyone, but I don't see any alternative. I just wish I'd gotten on to Johnston sooner. . . . The last time Brad and I were down, the mares' barn was spotless."

Ashleigh was frowning. "Mr. Townsend, I know you didn't want Wonder to leave Townsend Acres, but considering the circumstances, why don't I bring her to my parents' place. You know she'll get good care, and moving her would make less work when you're already shorthanded."

Mr. Townsend scowled and crossed his arms

127

over his chest. "I know how you feel, Ashleigh. Seeing these mares neglected makes my blood boil!" He clenched his hands into fists, then sighed. "I don't want her leaving Townsend Acres, but I suppose, under the circumstances, you're right. She's too valuable . . . and special. Moving her to your parents' is probably the sanest idea. And I know I can trust their expertise. Yes, all right," he agreed, "at least until we've hired a new manager and seen that he or she can do the job."

"Thanks, Mr. Townsend. I feel better being close to her, and now that she's in foal—"

"We don't want anything to happen to her," Mr. Townsend said. "Fine. You can use one of the farm vans to bring her over." Then he turned and left to check on the other mares.

"I understand why you're moving her," Samantha said with a heavy heart, "but I'm going to miss her."

Ashleigh nodded sadly, then laid her cheek against Wonder's neck. "At least I won't have to worry about you anymore, girl. You'll be with me." Then she straightened and said, "I'll go and get the van ready. Maybe one of the grooms can drive it over and back. I have my car here."

Samantha walked over to Wonder with tears in her eyes. "I really *am* going to miss you," she murmured to the mare. "But Ashleigh's right to move you. You'll be happier, and I can always come visit you there." Wonder whickered. The

mare was relaxing now that she had loving people around her and food and water. "Nothing's
the same around here anymore, is it, girl?"
Samantha said unhappily. "And there might be
more bad news to come."

10

"TOWNSEND AND HIS SON HAD A REAL SHOUTING MATCH last night," Charlie told Samantha and Yvonne as they led Pride up to the track early the next morning. The beautiful young colt didn't understand the bleak situation around the farm, or that his own life could soon be changing. He was frisky and full of high spirits, prancing over the grass and playfully nudging Samantha. She affectionately rubbed her hand along his neck.

"Townsend really laced into Brad," Charlie continued. "Seems he put Brad in charge of keeping an eye on the breeding manager and the operation down there."

Yvonne's eyes widened as she cast Samantha a sidelong glance.

Did Brad know *she* was the one who had raised

the alarm? Samantha wondered. If he didn't, he'd find out soon enough from stable talk. And knowing Brad, he'd hold it against her.

"I know what you're thinking," Yvonne said.

Samantha grimaced. She had enough to worry about without having to be concerned about Brad. "What are we doing this morning, Charlie?" she asked, changing the subject. "Do you still want to work him from a standing start?"

"Yup. He's ready. We can work him alone today. I see Maddock hasn't got his two-year-olds out yet."

As usual, Pride was quick to learn what Samantha wanted of him. After she'd warmed him up at a jog, she stopped him at the mile marker pole and visualized an imaginary line across the track. She readied herself, crouching in the saddle, hands firm on the reins at either side of Pride's neck. She glanced to the side of the track and waited until Charlie dropped his hand. Then she slid her hands forward on Pride's neck, tightened her heels, and yelled "Go!"

The colt hesitated for the briefest second, then shot forward at a gallop. She let him gallop an eighth of a mile, then slowed him, turned, and rode back to the mile marker to do it again. The second time Pride was off even more sharply. From the corner of her eye she saw Charlie's nod as she let Pride settle in to gallop out the rest of the mile. She praised him lavishly as they came off the track, and the colt seemed to know he'd done a good job.

Samantha was feeling exhilarated as she and Yvonne led Pride back to the barn. When she was working him around the oval, she could forget all the problems at the farm. Riding a horse like Pride was an experience not every rider had, and Samantha knew just how lucky she was.

She untacked the colt and threw a light sheet over him, then she and Yvonne walked him under the trees. The March air was cool enough that the colt hadn't worked up much of a sweat. In fact he acted like he hadn't been worked at all, prancing between them, tossing his elegant head.

All three of them enjoyed the walk, and when they returned to the barn, Samantha led Pride into his stall for breakfast and a grooming.

Yvonne offered to help some of the grooms with their chores, and when Pride was finished, Samantha went to Goddess's stall to check her feed and groom her for the morning.

She'd just started brushing Goddess's gleaming, nearly black coat when a voice interrupted her. "If I were you, I'd stop sticking my nose where it doesn't belong."

Samantha swung around to see Brad at the stall door. His handsome face was marred by an angry scowl.

"If you're talking about the broodmare barn, somebody had to do something," she said firmly.

"It would have been taken care of without *you* butting in."

132

"When?" Samantha shot back. "The barn was disgusting. The mares didn't have food or water. And Johnston was drunk."

"What goes on in the breeding area is none of your business. So stay out of it!" Brad walked off, leaving Samantha with an angry retort on the tip of her tongue.

"Jerk!" she said through gritted teeth. How she would love to tell him off! It was *his* fault that Johnston had gotten so lax. "He doesn't have the guts to take responsibility, so he blames it on me," she muttered to Goddess.

Goddess turned from her hay net and snorted.

"Right. That's what I think of him too!"

From then on, Samantha stayed as far out of Brad's way as she could, although it was impossible to avoid him totally. He hadn't made any more nasty remarks to her, but she could tell from his attitude that he was still sore about the broodmare barn incident. She noticed, too, that he watched Pride's workouts very intently, and she wondered what he had on his mind. Had Myron Yeakel been in touch with the Townsends again?

Samantha asked Charlie if he'd heard any rumors. "Nope," he answered, "and it doesn't pay to worry about things before they happen. Let's just concentrate on this colt's training."

And they did. By early April, Pride had progressed to the starting gate. With patience they had taught him not to fear entering the four-horse training gate. First, they led him through one of the narrow gate slots, with its front and back swinging doors open, until he was familiar with the apparatus. Then Samantha rode him through at a walk. When he seemed comfortable with that, she rode him in with the front doors closed, made him stand until Charlie triggered the gate release, then urged him forward quickly out of the gate.

"Not every trainer takes so many steps to break a young horse to the gate," Charlie told her, "but it pays off in the end. You're less likely to have a spooked, rearing horse on the track."

After Pride had become used to the gate, they started timing him for short gallops. Samantha didn't need a stopwatch to know the colt burned up the track. All she had to do was look at the faces of the trainers and other riders as they flew by. They all gawked in amazement.

Samantha knew that Pride shone compared to the other horses in training—with the exception of Goddess, who stood out among the older horses. Ashleigh had the filly's training moving smoothly forward. She was pointing Goddess toward a late-April race at Keeneland, and if she came out of it well, they would be heading toward the big national graded stakes races. Everyone had high hopes for the filly's four-year-old season. The only problem was that Townsend Acres didn't own the most promising older horse on the grounds, and it irked Brad no end.

"I wish he'd just leave me alone," Ashleigh growled one morning before Goddess was set to work. "I try to ignore him, but I know he can't stand my being here. I can feel the tension, and I'm afraid it's going to start getting to Goddess too."

"It hasn't so far," Charlie said. "And there's nothing Brad can do. Townsend has no problems with the filly being here, and you're sure paying enough for her keep."

"It just wears me down after a while," Ashleigh said.

"Try not to think about it," Charlie said. "So, how's Wonder settling in at your place?"

Ashleigh smiled. "She loves it. She seems perfectly content. We had the vet in to check her over yesterday, and he said she's one hundred percent healthy. He doesn't think she'll lose this foal. But, you know, it really bothers me that I still don't know what Mr. Townsend is going to do with his interest."

"You're not the only one," Samantha said.

"Well, there's one piece of good news," Charlie said.

"Oh?" both girls answered.

"Hear they've found a new breeding manager. Townsend hired him himself. A young fella, married, but his wife won't be working at the farm. Hear he comes with good references. Won't be starting for another month, though."

Ashleigh seemed relieved by the last piece of information, and Samantha knew it was because she wanted to keep Wonder at the Griffen farm for as long as possible. "At least when Mr. Townsend's around, things are better here," Ashleigh said.

"Yup, but he's heading north on another business trip," Charlie said.

Both girls groaned, and Samantha felt a twinge of fear. Was he going north to talk to Yeakel? she wondered.

Later, as Samantha walked Pride to cool him out, she tried to picture her life on the farm without him to care for and help train. "Oh, big guy," she said to the colt, "I don't know what I'd do without you. I'd be miserable, wondering who's taking care of you, if they're treating you right, how your training is going. . . ."

Pride lowered his head to scratch his cheek against her shoulder and huffed out a sweet breath.

"Yeah, I love you too," she said with a sigh.

Mr. Townsend left, leaving Brad in charge, and the atmosphere around the farm changed immediately. Brad was obnoxious and arrogant, and he liked to tell all the stable hands how to do their jobs. Even the episode with Johnston hadn't put a stop to his bossiness, and his father wasn't there to keep him in line.

136

A few nights after Mr. Townsend's departure, Mr. McLean came home looking tired and very depressed.

"Is something wrong, Dad?" Samantha asked over dinner.

He looked up distractedly. "No, nothing for you to worry about."

"I know things have been getting worse around here since Mr. Townsend left."

"Yes, that's true," her father admitted. "I guess that's plain for anyone to see."

Samantha waited for him to say more. When he didn't, she prodded him further. "Dad, tell me. It's not just the usual stuff, is it?"

He looked up at her and hesitated. "Well, I guess you have the right to know," he finally said. "I'm worried because I don't know if I'll have a job here much longer."

Samantha leaned back in her chair in shock. "Why do you say that?"

"It's no secret that Brad Townsend and I don't get along . . ."

"Yes," Samantha breathed.

"He's always interfered with the training, and we've had some pretty heavy disagreements about training procedures."

"Charlie says Brad thinks he knows more than he does."

"That's very true, and since his father left, he's taken away several of my horses to train himself—

137

not that I've been left with that many to begin with, compared to last year."

Samantha felt a stab of fear. "Can't Maddock do anything?"

"Well, he's told me he likes the job I've been doing. I've brought around a couple of horses no one thought would lift a hoof, but there isn't a lot Maddock can do. He's told Brad to leave the training to me—that his father is happy with the situation the way it is—but you can't tell that Townsend kid anything."

"Mr. Townsend would *never* fire you!" Samantha exclaimed.

"Not on the grounds of my performance," her father said, "but it make me nervous the way they're cutting staff. And Brad has the authority to lay me off."

"Oh, Dad!" Samantha cried.

He laid his hand over hers. "See, I shouldn't have told you. It's probably not as bad as I'm imagining. Forget I said anything."

But of course Samantha couldn't forget. She was frightened, because she knew Brad was capable of laying her father off. Or maybe he would make life miserable enough for her father that he would resign. And Clay Townsend wasn't there to intercede.

When they were finished eating, her father collected the dishes. "Go on and do your homework," he said. "I'll clean up."

Samantha hesitated for a moment, then gathered her books from the table near the door and went into her room. She heard the low volume of the television set as her father switched it on to watch the news. She closed the door behind her, carried her books to the bed, then picked up the phone to call Yvonne.

"Hi there!" Yvonne said cheerfully when she answered. In the background Samantha heard loud rap music. "My parents aren't home and my brother has his CD player turned way up," Yvonne explained. "Let me shut the door." The noise subsided, and Yvonne came back to the phone. "So, what's up?"

"I just wanted to talk to someone," Samantha said. "My father came home tonight all depressed. He's afraid he might lose his job."

"That can't be," Yvonne said. "He's such a good trainer!"

"I know, but Brad's been making it hard for him to do his job." Samantha sighed. "He told me to forget he said anything, but all I have to do is think about leaving here and I feel sick. I don't want to go back to moving from track to track. I've been so happy on the farm, even if things have been rough lately."

"I don't want you to move either! And I don't think you will. Mr. Townsend will be back soon. He'll straighten it out."

"Well, the other thing that scares me is that

Brad might try to interfere with Pride's training. If he's taking over other horses—and Pride's doing so well. . . ."

"I guess I'd be scared about that too if I were you. But I don't think you should worry. Charlie and Ashleigh wouldn't let him!"

"No, I suppose not. And besides, that's the least of my problems. I mean, we still don't know if Mr. Townsend's going to sell his interest." Samantha bit her lip to stop herself from crying. "Yvonne, what would I do if he does?" she said in a choked voice.

"Oh, Sammy, don't be upset," Yvonne said, trying to console her. "He'll decide to keep his interest. You'll see. And everything will turn out all right."

Samantha took a deep breath and tried to think of something else to talk about. Finally she said, "How'd your lesson go this afternoon?"

"Incredible! I did a whole course of jumps in the ring without one fault."

"Good for you," Samantha said, brightening. "And now that the weather's nice, you can come over and do some trail riding with me again. Ashleigh wants me to take Pride out when I can to build up his stamina."

"You're on!" Yvonne said with enthusiasm. "I really love jumping in the ring, but it's so much fun to be outside. I don't suppose Dominator can jump," she added speculatively.

Samantha laughed. "I'm sure he can—but I'm certainly *not* going to let Pride do any jumping. I can't risk injuring him. Ashleigh and Charlie would have a fit."

"Okay, so we won't go jumping," Yvonne said. "I was just thinking."

"Yeah, I bet you were," Samantha teased. "See you tomorrow."

When she had hung up, Samantha rolled over on the bed and flipped open her algebra book. She started to read, but couldn't concentrate. It was at times like this that she really missed her mother. They used to be able to talk for hours, and her mother was always there when Samantha needed her most. She'd had the magical talent of making even the worst situation seem not so bad after all.

The page grew blurry, and Samantha blinked back her tears. Something good had to happen soon. If only Mr. Townsend would come back from his trip, send Brad to Brazil to run a farm down there, and tell her and Ashleigh that he'd found the money to keep his interest in Wonder and Pride.

Samantha smiled. Now that was a nice thought!

11

ASHLEIGH STORMED OUT OF GODDESS'S STABLE A WEEK
later and strode over to Samantha, who was sitting
on a bench cleaning Pride's tack. "I hate to tell you
this, Sammy," she said angrily, "but I'm taking
Goddess out of here."

Samantha straightened and stared at Ashleigh.

"I've had it up to here with Brad Townsend!"
Ashleigh yelled, slashing her hand across her forehead. "We just had another huge fight about
Goddess being here. What does he want from me?
I'm paying for her feed and her board now, too,
and I give them part of her winnings! I just can't
take it anymore!"

"I guess I'm not surprised," Samantha whispered, feeling a lump in her throat. "You're going
to take her to Mike's?"

Ashleigh nodded. "I'll bring her over in the van this afternoon. He's got the room and the training oval. I wanted to keep Goddess and Pride in the same place, but I guess it's not going to work. This means I'll have to be at Mike's nearly every morning to work Goddess, so I won't have time to get over here too. But I trust you and Charlie to do a good job with Pride."

"We will," Samantha promised. "He almost trains himself. But I'm going to miss Goddess!"

"I know, and I'm sorry," Ashleigh said. "You've been great with her, a huge help, especially when I hurt my neck a year ago and couldn't ride. I know we wouldn't have been able to race in October if you hadn't filled in."

"Exercise riding her was one of the best things that ever happened to me."

"You can visit her at Mike's place anytime, though I know it won't be the same." Ashleigh shook her head. "Nothing's the same anymore, is it? Wonder at our place, Goddess at Mike's, and Pride here. I wish I knew what was going to happen."

"So do I," Samantha said.

Later that afternoon, Samantha watched as Mike and Ashleigh pulled into the stable yard with a van.

"Not the greatest couple of months, huh?" Mike said, coming over to her. "How are you holding up?"

Samantha shrugged. "Hanging in there, I guess. It's getting pretty awful, though. If Pride goes too . . ."

"I know," he said, quickly squeezing her shoulders. "Ash is a mess over it."

As Ashleigh led Goddess from the barn Charlie, Hank, and several of the grooms were in the stable yard, looking glum. Charlie walked up to give the filly's shoulder a last pat. He spoke to Ashleigh and the filly, though Samantha couldn't hear what he was saying. When he turned away, he pulled his hat down over his scowling brows.

Samantha felt her own eyes welling with tears. This would be the last time she saw Goddess at Townsend Acres.

"Why don't you ride with us when we take her over?" Mike suggested to her gently. "You haven't seen Whitebrook yet, and either Ashleigh or I can give you a ride home later."

Samantha looked up and nodded quickly. She was afraid she'd lose it when she said good-bye to the filly, and she didn't want to break down in front of everybody. "Let me just tell my father."

Mr. McLean, who had joined the other staff in the yard, immediately nodded when Samantha asked him if she could go. "It'll be good for you to get out of here," he said. "I'll see you later."

As they rode through the rolling countryside to Mike's place, Samantha looked out at the landscape and tried to put aside some of her sadness.

Spring had turned the fields a lush, fragile green, and daffodils bloomed on the sides of the road. The white-fenced paddocks of horse country spread out for miles, it seemed, and the air was fresh with the scent of new grass.

A while later Mike pulled into a gravel drive marked with a modest sign that said WHITEBROOK FARM. "Here it is," he said to Samantha. "Not much compared to Townsend Acres, but I'm proud of it."

"And you should be," Ashleigh said. "Mike and his father only bought the farm a few years ago," she explained to Samantha. "I think they've come a long way."

"It looks good to me," Samantha said. Ahead on the left of the drive was a white farmhouse, and on the opposite side there were three barns, several outbuildings, and a training oval. Beyond the buildings were the paddocks, where a half-dozen Thoroughbreds grazed. Whitebrook was small and modest compared to Townsend Acres, but everything was clean and obviously well cared for.

Mike parked the van close to the barns, and as soon as he did an old black man hurried over from a stable building. He started unlatching the back of the van as they all climbed out.

"Thanks, Len," Mike said with a smile. "I don't think you've met Samantha McLean. She's been helping Ashleigh and Charlie train Goddess and Wonder's Pride."

Len gave Samantha a wide grin. "Glad to meet you. I've heard about all the good work you've done with the filly and that colt."

Samantha smiled. It really was good to be away from Townsend Acres for a while, she thought. It was such a relief to escape all the tension.

"Charlie Burke and I go back a long way," Len added. "We both started working at the tracks when we were in our twenties—and that *was* a long time ago." He laughed. "Let's get this filly out of here. I've got a stall all set for her."

"Len's in charge of our stables," Mike explained to Samantha. "He came to Kentucky with my father and me when we bought the farm."

Len climbed the ramp into the one-horse van and started backing Goddess out. As soon as she was clear, she lifted her head and looked around.

"Yeah, girl, I know it's a strange place, but you're going to like it here," Ashleigh said. "Come on, let's get you settled in your new stall." She took Goddess's lead and patted her neck.

Len led the way into the largest of the barns, where six roomy box stalls ran up and down each side of the aisle. He had readied one in the middle. Ashleigh brought Goddess in, and the filly walked across the thick, fresh bedding and circled the stall. It didn't take her long to find the hay net, and she quickly swiped a mouthful.

"Looks like she'll settle in fine," Len said. "I'll stay and talk to her for a while."

"Thanks, Len," Ashleigh said. "Mike and I want to show Samantha around."

As they headed off down the aisle, Mike pointed out the horses he had in training—two fillies and three colts. "I think you saw Moondrone run," he said, motioning to the compact bay.

"I did," Samantha said, "when Goddess ran last fall at Keeneland. Do you have him back in training?"

"Yes. I might decide to race him at Churchill Downs in May, or maybe I'll wait and bring him up to New York when Belmont opens."

Next Mike led them through the two other barns. One housed his three stallions, including Jazzman, a beautiful black that had done incredibly well for Mike at the track. Mike had retired him the past summer, and this spring was his first stud season.

"I'll bet his stud book was full," Samantha said.

Mike smiled. "I can't complain. We didn't pay much for him, but his record at the track was so good, we had plenty of interest. I can't wait for his first crop of foals next spring." They moved on to the next stall. "This is Indigo," he said. "He never did as well as Jazzman at the track, but I think he'll have some nice offspring. And this bay is Maxwell. He never raced, but we liked his bloodlines and bought him strictly for stud. His first crop of yearlings is out in the paddock."

Mike led them on into the last of the barns,

where his half-dozen broodmares were stabled. One had recently foaled, and Samantha looked over the stall door to see a fuzzy brown bundle with spindly legs nuzzling up to its dam. The three-day-old foal turned its head at the sound of their voices and took a few steps toward them, its oversize ears flopping back and forth.

Samantha smiled, thinking of Pride when he was a foal.

"He's one of Maxwell's," Mike said. "It's early to tell, but I have a lot of hopes for him. His dam is a Secretariat mare, and Secretariat is known to be an outstanding broodmare sire."

Samantha studied the dark chestnut mare. Just about everyone knew of Secretariat, the Triple Crown winner and multiple champion, even people who never paid any attention to horse racing. No recent Thoroughbred racehorse had yet surpassed Secretariat's amazing achievements.

"So you're going to keep him and train him?" Samantha asked. "I plan to," Mike said. "It'll be pretty exciting racing a horse I bred myself."

From the broodmare barn, they walked out along the paddocks, and Mike pointed out two small cottages. "Len has that one by the barns. My father and I just finished fixing up the other one, so it'll be ready for when we decide we can afford more staff, which might be pretty soon."

Samantha thought about the problems at Townsend Acres. Mike and Ashleigh's parents seemed to be expanding their operations, so why was Townsend Acres doing so poorly? "Why do you think Townsend Acres is having so many financial problems?" she asked Mike.

"I'd say they overexpanded—bought too much expensive stock and maybe borrowed money to do it. Then they had a couple of not-so-great racing years, and also auction prices went way down." He shrugged. "That's just a guess."

When Ashleigh dropped her back at Townsend Acres just before dinner, Samantha went straight to Pride's stall. As usual he was glad to see her and whickered a happy welcome. She let her eyes linger on the beautiful animal—his sleek, well-muscled body, his arched neck, his long, silky mane and tail, his elegant head, the look of bright intelligence in his eyes. She went into the stall and hugged him.

"You're the last one left," she told him softly. "And I might lose you, too. I can't stand to think of it."

The next morning Yvonne was waiting by Samantha's locker. "Ashleigh took Fleet Goddess to Mike's yesterday afternoon," Samantha told Yvonne.

Yvonne's cheery smile disappeared. "She did? That's awful, Sammy. What are you going to do?"

Samantha shrugged. "There's not much I *can* do. I know Ashleigh didn't have a choice. I mean,

149

Brad's always on her case. But I'll miss Goddess terribly."

"You still have Pride, though."

"For now, anyway," Samantha said miserably.

As Samantha made her way to homeroom, she saw Tor approaching from the opposite direction. He smiled and waved, then threaded through the crowd in the hall toward her.

"I just read your last article in the newspaper," he said. "I thought it was great. Too bad you're not an expert on jumping. The stable could use the extra publicity."

"Thanks," Samantha said, smiling. "I'm glad you liked it. I have fun writing the columns. Maybe you could ask Yvonne to write about the riding stable—or why don't you give it a shot yourself?"

"Hey, that's an idea," he said. "Only, I'm not really sure I'm any good at writing stuff like that."

"How's the show jumping going?" she asked.

Tor walked with her to the door of her homeroom and told her about his heavy training schedule and his plans for Top Hat. "Maybe I'll see you over at the stable with Yvonne," he said.

"Yeah, I'll try to come over soon, but things have been pretty crazy."

"See you, then." He waved as Samantha turned and slipped into her homeroom.

She'd no sooner sat down than Maureen was at her desk. "I have a great idea," she said. "Why don't you write your next column about that colt you're training?"

"Pride?"

"Yeah, I think it would be great."

"Really?" Samantha said. "Boy, I sure could write about Pride!"

"Good. Then do it," Maureen said with a smile. "The only problem is that we're going to need the piece pretty early this time. Could you get it done by next week?"

"If I'm writing about Pride," Samantha said confidently, "I *know* I can."

Maureen laughed. "Okay, I'm counting on you!"

12

"I WANT TO BREEZE HIM THREE FURLONGS," CHARLIE SAID to Samantha a week later as she brought Pride out to the oval. "I'll be clocking him," Charlie added. "I'd like to see him average about twelve seconds per furlong. The colt should be able to do it without you pushing him at all, especially after what we've seen earlier this week."

Samantha fastened the chin strap of her helmet and nodded. They'd been working Pride up to longer and longer breezes, sometimes alone, sometimes with other two-year-olds. Not only had he effortlessly demonstrated speed, he'd blown by the other two-year-olds as if they were standing still. Everyone had been staring in awe when Samantha had proudly ridden him off the track. Samantha smiled now, thinking of it.

"He can probably do better than twelve seconds a furlong," she said.

"Yup, but we don't want to push him too hard too soon."

"Right." Samantha turned toward Pride in preparation for mounting. But before Charlie could clasp his hands together to give her a boost into the saddle, Brad Townsend walked up.

"I want to get a feel for this colt's action myself," Brad told them arrogantly. "I'll take him out this morning."

Samantha's heart plummeted to her feet. This was what she'd been afraid of.

"I don't think you will," Charlie said quietly.

"What are you talking about?" Brad snapped. "I'll take out any horse I want. Myron Yeakel is very interested in buying out our half-interest in this colt, and I want to know exactly what we've got. Besides, I think you should be working him longer distances by now. He's ready for a half-mile breeze."

Samantha saw a dangerous gleam in Charlie's eyes. The old trainer was not going to let Brad interfere. "First of all," he said in a low but firm voice, "your father hasn't told us that he's decided to sell. There's a good chance he won't. Secondly, I'm not letting *anyone* interfere with Pride's training. The colt's doing too well. He'll be ready to race by the end of May."

"Remember who you work for, Charlie," Brad

warned. "I'm in charge as long as my father's not here, and I'll make the decisions."

"You've got that wrong," Charlie answered. "In this case I'm working for the colt's other owner. Unless Ashleigh tells me otherwise, I'll make the training decisions."

"I'm riding him," Brad said, furious that Charlie dared to question him.

Samantha's skin crawled just *thinking* of Brad in the saddle of her beloved colt. The day before, the horse Brad had been exercising came off the track limping. "Pushed him too hard," Charlie had said. "Shouldn't have breezed him that extra furlong." The horse's injury hadn't been serious, but he'd had to come out of training.

Pride threw up his head and eyed Brad in confusion, then he nervously danced his hindquarters in an arc over the grass. Brad reached out and took the colt's reins.

Samantha couldn't stand by silently another second. She didn't care about the consequences. She was *not* going to let Brad get in Pride's saddle! She took a step forward.

"Samantha!" Her father's voice pierced the anger that clouded her brain. She stopped, startled, and saw her father motion her to stay put. Then he confronted Brad directly. He was as tall as Brad, but bigger boned. "I wouldn't do that if I were you," he said with deadly calm. "I'd listen to Charlie."

Brad swung his head around and stared at Samantha's father as if the older man had suddenly grown two heads. "What are you talking about?" he said with a laugh. "Who are you to tell me what to do? When I say I'm riding this colt, I'm riding this colt. I'm already pretty unhappy with the way you've been training, McLean. I wouldn't push it." Brad turned away and pulled down a stirrup to mount.

Samantha saw her father clench his hands at his side. "Like I said, I'd listen to Charlie."

Brad looked back, but when he saw the expression on Mr. McLean's face, his own paled a little. "You're out of line, McLean." But Brad's tone wasn't as arrogant as it had been earlier.

"No, I'm not. As far as I'm concerned, you've bullied people around long enough, and I'm not going to stand by and let you take advantage of Charlie—the best trainer on these grounds."

Brad's mouth tightened, and an angry flush rose on his cheeks.

Then Maddock walked up to stand beside Samantha's father. "I'd suggest you do what he says," he said quietly.

Samantha stared at him. Maddock was taking sides with her father against the owner's son? Samantha had been sure that Maddock would either stay out of it or remain loyal to Townsend Acres.

"Have you all lost it?" Brad said, gaping at

Maddock. "Have you forgotten who's in charge around here?"

"No, I haven't forgotten who's in charge," Maddock said calmly. "Your father. And I don't think your father wants anyone interfering with the job Charlie is doing with this colt. Charlie Burke has more experience and knowledge in his pinky than you have in your whole body."

Brad's expression was livid. Samantha had never seen anyone look so angry. From the corner of her eye, she saw Charlie's mouth twitch in the tiniest of smiles, and his blue eyes were now twinkling.

Brad glared at Samantha's father, looking for an outlet for his fury. "You're fired!" he cried. "Get off this farm today!"

Samantha gasped, but her father just gave Brad a level look. "I'd be delighted. No job is worth putting up with what's been going on around here lately."

Brad swung around, turning to Charlie next. "And we'll see about this colt!"

"I'm sure your father will want to hear all the details when he gets back here tonight," Maddock said mildly.

Brad's eyes widened in surprise. "What—"

Maddock cut him short. "He called this morning. You weren't around, so I talked to him. His plans have changed. He'll be flying into Lexington tonight."

Without another word, Brad stormed off toward the stable.

"I appreciate your support," Charlie said to Mr. McLean. "Didn't want you to lose your job over it, though."

Samantha walked over to her father, and he put an arm around her shoulders and squeezed them. "Sorry, Sammy. I guess I put my foot in it this time. I know how you love this place, but I just couldn't stand by."

"It's all right, Dad. I'm glad you told him off."

"I wouldn't start packing my bags yet," Maddock said. "I don't think Townsend will want to lose you."

Mr. McLean ran a hand through his hair. "I don't know if I want to stay after all of this. Things will be pretty unpleasant around here."

"I know how you feel," Maddock said, "but think about it. I've sure been pleased with the job you're doing. At least wait till Townsend gets back tonight and talk to him."

"I suppose we'll do that," Mr. McLean said wearily. "We don't have anyplace to go anyway."

"I'll stand behind you," Charlie added. "I'll make sure Townsend hears both sides of the story."

"Thanks."

"Well," Charlie said, pushing back his hat and scowling. "Guess there's nothing to do now but get

157

a work into this colt. You feel up to it?" he asked Samantha.

Samantha straightened. It was just beginning to sink in that Brad had fired her father, that they might have to leave Townsend Acres—that this might be the last chance she had to work Pride! But she couldn't think about that . . . not now. She lifted her chin. "I'm ready."

Pride had quieted down a little, but he was still more high-strung than usual. Samantha soothed him with her voice as she settled in his saddle and picked up the reins.

"Remember what I told you earlier," Charlie said.

"Yes," she said softly. "Okay, Pride, let's go."

Once on the oval, Samantha warmed up the colt at a trot and a canter. Every eye was on them, but Pride would put in a good performance. She was more worried about her own concentration. Her stomach was knotted in a ball, and she was furious with Brad. "Think about it later," she told herself. "Pride's work is too important." She urged the colt into a slow gallop and put all else from her mind. The colt moved with fluid grace up the backstretch and toward the far turn. The chorus of Pride's snorted breaths and pounding hooves was music in her ears. The rail posts whizzed by, and she still hadn't let him out. She saw the three-eighths pole ahead, but waited patiently until they'd reached it. Then she slid her hands forward along Pride's neck, giving him rein. He needed no other encouragement. He instantly changed gears, and they were flying! She was one with him, moving with the motion of his long strides as they roared along over the dirt.

They flashed past the line, and Samantha stood in the stirrups, signaling Pride to slow down. He dropped back into a canter, then a trot, and she circled him toward the gap. His neck was arched against the rein as he pranced off the track.

"Oh, wow!" Samantha gasped. "Oh, Pride, that was perfect—absolutely perfect!" She was exhilarated from the ride.

There were smiles on the faces of those who'd been watching.

Charlie walked over to take Pride's head. "Thirty-five seconds and a tick," he said. "He did the last furlong in eleven seconds. And he wasn't even trying."

"It was good," Samantha said.

"Yup." Charlie nodded. "It was good."

Samantha leaned forward and hugged the colt's neck. "Pride, you're just incredible!"

But once she'd unsaddled the colt and started walking him to cool him out, reality settled in again. Her stomach knotted and her smile slipped from her face. After she'd led Pride around for a few minutes, Samantha put him in his stall and gave him a light brushing. The horse didn't understand what going on, but he must have sensed Saman-tha's sadness. He whickered softly and blew soft breaths in her mane of red hair. "Oh, boy," she cried, "when are things going to start getting better?"

When she was about to leave the stall, her father showed up. "Sammy," he said softly, "I'm so sorry about the way things turned out. I couldn't stop myself. I was just so angry."

"I know how you felt, Dad," Samantha said. "If you hadn't stopped me, I was going to tackle him."

"I kind of guessed that was on your mind when I saw the look on your face."

For a second, they both smiled. Then her father added, "I don't want you to worry yourself sick over this. I'm going to wait and talk to Townsend. Maddock is right—I don't think he'll go along with firing me, but you never know." He shrugged. "Sammy, I don't want to take you away from here, but do you understand that I might not have any choice? And staying here when there are hard feelings between me and Brad might not work either."

"Don't worry, Dad. I understand."

"Thanks, sweetheart." Her father gave her a warm smile, then said, "You'd better get going or you'll be late for school."

Samantha quickly changed for school and ran

160

for the bus. Where would she and her father go if they had to leave Townsend Acres? she wondered desperately. Would they move out of Lexington? Would she have to leave behind the friends she'd made? If they left the farm, she'd be forced to stop working with Ashleigh and Charlie. And worst of all, she'd have to leave Pride behind.

Yvonne and Maureen were waiting in the hall near Samantha's locker. Samantha had brought with her the finished article about Pride's training. When she'd finished writing the final draft the night before, she'd been really happy with it. Now she wondered if she'd even be in Lexington to write the next.

"Uh-oh," Yvonne said when she saw Samantha's white face. "What's wrong?"

Samantha swallowed. Her throat felt so tight, she didn't know if she could get the words out, but haltingly she explained that Brad had fired her father.

"Oh, no!" Yvonne exclaimed. "This is serious!"

Samantha nodded. "Yes, it is," she said hoarsely.

Maureen was staring at her from behind her thick glasses. "You really think you'll have to move?"

"We'll find out tonight." Samantha opened her bag and took out three neatly written sheets of paper. "The article on Pride," she said, handing it over.

"You finished it. Great!" Maureen said. "I can't wait to read it."

The bell rang, and Maureen slipped the article into her notebook. "I still have to go to my locker," she said, backing away from them. "I'll read this in study hall and see you guys at lunch. Bye!" She turned and ran down the hall.

"Oh, Sammy, I don't know what to say," Yvonne murmured.

"I guess there's nothing *anyone* can do right now. We'll just have to wait until my father talks to Mr. Townsend."

Samantha was in a fog through most of her morning classes. Her thoughts kept straying over the past two years since she and her father had moved to Townsend Acres. She'd never lived in one place for so long, and she'd never had so many good friends. She thought of Pride's fantastic workout that morning, and the awful scene with Brad, and knew she could be separated from the colt even if Mr. Townsend decided not to sell his interest.

At lunch, as Samantha was silently toying with her food, Maureen came hurrying up to her.

"I read it," Maureen said breathlessly as she slid in next to Yvonne and Samantha. "It's great—fantastic. You make it all so interesting! Have you ever thought of becoming a writer?"

Maureen's enthusiasm jarred Samantha out of her thoughts. "Actually, no. I usually think about becoming a jockey, maybe a trainer."

"Well, you could do both!" Maureen said with excitement.

In spite of herself, Samantha smiled. "I suppose I could," she said. *But first I've got to get the rest of my life sorted out.*

13

SAMANTHA CAME HOME AFTER SCHOOL THAT DAY AND followed her usual routine. She dropped off her books on the table by the door, then went up to her room to change into her work jeans and boots. As she was pulling on her socks, it suddenly hit her that soon her room might not be her room anymore and that the apartment might not be their home.

Her eyes caught on the photograph of her mother, and her throat tightened so that she could hardly breathe. She quickly put on her boots and rushed out of the apartment into the sunny stable yard, where she stood for several seconds pulling deep breaths into her lungs.

Charlie was sitting on a bench, enjoying the warm spring sun. He looked at her from under his shaggy brows, then motioned for her to come over.

"You know, sometimes things look pretty black," Charlie said when Samantha sat beside him. "But you should never give up hope."

"I haven't . . . yet," Samantha said haltingly.

"Townsend will be back. He'll sort things out. Don't pay any attention to that son of his." Charlie paused and adjusted the brim of his hat. "Townsend and I have had our differences over the years, but he's a decent sort. He'll do his best by your father."

Samantha looked at the old trainer and sighed. "I hope you're right."

Mr. Townsend still hadn't returned by dinnertime, and Samantha was so anxious, she couldn't eat.

"Ashleigh came and thanked me for looking out for Pride," her father said as they sat down at the table. "I appreciated it. I know she's got a lot on her plate, too."

"She was upset about what Brad did," Samantha said without looking up.

Her father watched as she pushed her food around her plate. "I know how you feel," he said, "but at least drink your milk."

Samantha nodded and picked up her glass.

When they were clearing the table a few minutes later, there was a knock on the door. Samantha froze, knowing that it would be Mr. Townsend, then walked across the room to open it.

"Hello, Sammy," he said. "Is your father here?"

"Yes. Come in, Mr. Townsend." Samantha stood back and pulled the door open. Mr. Townsend stepped into the small kitchen–living room.

"Hello, Ian," Mr. Townsend said. "Maddock told me what happened this morning, and I don't think I need to tell you how upset I am."

Samantha slipped into her bedroom, but left the door open a crack so she could hear them talk. She sat on the edge of her bed and clasped her hands tightly in her lap.

"I can explain why I—" her father began.

"No, I'm not upset with you," Mr. Townsend said quickly. "I'm upset with my son. He reacted rashly. I guess he still has a lot to learn." He paused. "Needless to say, I don't want you to leave the farm. You're a valuable employee, and Ken Maddock has only had good things to say about you. Ian, I'd like to ask that you forget what was said this morning."

"I'd like to do that," Mr. McLean said, "but when something like this happens, there are usually hard feelings left over, and working conditions don't improve."

Samantha cringed. Her father was going to say no.

"I understand what you're saying," Townsend said, "and I feel responsible for some of the confusion since I've been away so much this year. But I'd hate to lose you."

166

There was a moment's silence. Samantha knew her father was sorting things through in his mind. *Say yes, Dad,* she silently pleaded.

"I appreciate your coming to talk to me," Mr. McLean finally said. "For the most part, I've enjoyed working here. . . . But I need to think about it—if you'll let me."

"I was afraid of that," Mr. Townsend said glumly. "After what's happened, though, I understand. Please give it some serious thought, and until you make a decision, I'll consider your status as it was—assistant trainer."

"Thank you. I'll make my decision as soon as I can. I won't keep you hanging."

"I'd appreciate that."

Samantha was close to tears. All her father had to do was say yes, and they could have definitely stayed—but he didn't!

As soon as she heard the door close, she rushed out of her bedroom. "Why did you say you'd have to think about it?" she cried.

"Because I do," her father said. "I don't have a problem at all with Mr. Townsend, but I can't see his son taking kindly to my staying here. Every time he looks at me, he'll be reminded of how he was humiliated in front of the entire staff. And he'll resent it."

Samantha listened to her father intently, trying to understand.

"That doesn't make for pleasant conditions," he

continued. "Sammy, as much as I want to make you happy, I can't go to work every day and do a good job when the situation around me is so tense."

"But Dad, I don't want to move again!" Samantha said desperately, too tired and frightened to keep her tears in check.

"Sweetheart, I don't want us to move either. I'll weigh everything before I decide, and I'll put out feelers for other jobs in Lexington. We might not have to leave the area. I know you've made friends here."

Her father took her into his arms as Samantha tried to bite back her sobs. It wasn't just the thought of leaving Lexington that was making her miserable—she would have to leave Pride, too, and all her dreams for him.

For the next few days, Samantha walked around like a zombie. The only time she could shake off her blues was when she was riding Pride on the training oval.

Ashleigh tried exercising the colt one morning and came off the track glowing. "He's everything you said, Sammy. He's a dream come true, and I have you to thank for a lot of it."

Later, as they walked Pride back to the stable, Ashleigh asked, "Has your father made up his mind about staying?"

"He's been making calls to other training farms," Samantha said, "but nobody's looking for help."

Some part of Samantha thought that was good news. After all, if there weren't any other openings, maybe her father would decide to stay at Townsend Acres.

"How's Brad been acting?" Ashleigh asked.

"He stays out of my way, but I'm beginning to understand what my father means about working conditions. I've seen the looks Brad gives my father—pretty awful. He doesn't interfere because his father's been around, but he hasn't forgotten. My dad doesn't look very happy."

"No, Brad wouldn't forget something like that," Ashleigh mused. "But I think I might have an answer for you."

Samantha looked over at the older girl. "What do you mean?"

Ashleigh smiled. "I can't tell you yet, but be patient, and I will soon."

Later that evening there was a knock on the McLeans' door. When Samantha opened it, she found Ashleigh and Mike standing on the doorstep. "Hi," she said in surprise. "What are you guys doing here?"

Ashleigh grinned. "We've got a proposition for your father." As they came inside, Mr. McLean stepped to the door of his bedroom, where he'd been working. He was just as surprised as Samantha to see Ashleigh and Mike.

"You two are over here late," he said. "Did you come to see Sammy? Make yourselves at home."

"Actually," Mike said, "I came to talk to you. I'd like to offer you a job."

Mr. McLean's eyes widened a little, but he stepped out of the bedroom and motioned Mike and Ashleigh toward the small living room. "What kind of job?" he asked when they were all seated.

"Well," Mike began, "I guess you know that my father and I have gradually been expanding at Whitebrook."

"Yes," Mr. McLean said, nodding.

"We've been doing pretty well, and we think we've reached the point where we need to hire more help," Mike went on. "We're going to start taking in other horses for training—particularly two-year-olds—and we need a trainer. Until I'm out of school, I can't do it all myself, and my father's gotten more interested in the breeding end. So we'd like you to come and work for us. There's a cottage on the property that goes with the position, which we've just fixed it up."

Samantha stared at Mike in surprise. When Ashleigh had told her about having a solution, Samantha hadn't thought about *this* possibility. She remembered the little cottage at Mike's, and she thought of the training oval and the well-kept stables. Her heart started beating a little faster with excitement.

"Well," Mr. McLean said, "you've sure caught me by surprise. I had no idea you would be looking for training help."

"We wanted to be absolutely certain that we were taking the right step," Mike said. "But we're positive now, and we would really like to have your help. We'll meet the salary Townsend's paying you."

Mr. McLean was shaking his head in bemusement. Then he frowned. "You're not by any chance offering me this job out of pity, knowing the situation here?"

"Absolutely not," Mike answered. "The timing just turned out to be right. We're ready to expand, and I think you're the best trainer for the job. That's the truth."

Samantha watched her father's face and saw him growing more receptive to the idea. "Exactly what would my responsibilities be?" Mr. McLean asked. "How many horses are we talking about, and how much control would I have?"

As he and Mike discussed the details, Samantha glanced over at Ashleigh, who gave her a subtle smile. Samantha crossed her fingers and returned the smile, but her father hadn't decided yet.

"I'd like to see your facilities."

"All right," Mike said, grinning. "I was going to suggest that you come over tomorrow or the next day."

"You'll like the place, Dad," Samantha said eagerly. In her thoughts, she was already cheering. She wouldn't have to leave her friends behind

171

after all! And she wouldn't be totally removed from Pride. Maybe she could even keep exercise riding him—if the Townsends didn't sell their interest.

"Okay, then," her father said. "We'll come over tomorrow and take a look. Is three thirty all right, after Sammy gets home from school?"

"I'll be there," Mike said.

14

MR. MCLEAN LIKED WHITEBROOK, AS SAMANTHA WAS
sure he would, but by Thursday he still hadn't made
up his mind about what he was going to do. It did
seem more and more likely that they would leave
Townsend Acres, though. Her father looked worn
and tired and totally fed up with the animosity Brad
still showed him.

"It's so hard not knowing what's going to happen," Samantha said to Yvonne at lunch one day.
"I guess my father needs time to make sure he's
doing the right thing. But I just wish he would
decide."

"I can imagine how you feel," Yvonne sympa-
thized. "I'd hate not knowing, and the job at
Mike's farm sounds so perfect—I mean, as perfect
as you can get if you have to leave Townsend

Acres. Not that it'll be the same—"

"But it's better than nothing." Samantha frowned and took a sip of juice. "I think Pride's starting to sense that things aren't right. I had a hard time getting him to settle in his workout this morning."

"Have you heard if Mr. Townsend's going to sell his interest?"

"No. I would've told you if I had. I try not to think about it, but I'm terrified and there's nothing I can do."

Yvonne bit her lip. "But he's still doing well, isn't he?"

"Oh, yeah. He's still amazing. If everything else wasn't such a mess, I'd be getting really excited about his first race, which is coming up soon."

After school Samantha met Maureen, and together they went to a newspaper staff meeting. Later on, Samantha's father picked her up to take her home.

"So how did it go?" he asked.

"Okay," Samantha said. "They're going to run my article on Pride as a feature. The issue comes out next week."

"Well!" her father said, smiling. "I can't wait to see it! I have a budding writer on my hands, eh?"

"I don't know about that, but I liked writing the piece."

A few moments later as they left the heavier congestion of the Lexington streets, Samantha's father said, "I've decided I'm going to take the job Mike's offered."

Samantha sat up straight and turned to her father. "You are! Oh, I'm so glad!"

"At first I was afraid Mike was offering me the job out of pity," he explained, "but the more I think about it, the more I like the prospect of working at Whitebrook. Mike and his father have good ideas, and there will always be something to dig my teeth into. And frankly, I don't see any chance of things working out at Townsend Acres. Townsend himself has been great, but I can feel Brad's resentment. It's just too uncomfortable."

Samantha nodded. "Yes, I know. I've seen the way he acts around you."

Her father went on. "I know you'll miss the place, but Ashleigh wants you to continue helping her with Pride, so maybe it won't be so bad. And you'll still be going to the same school."

"It's not so bad," Samantha told him firmly. "I like Whitebrook. If we have to move, I'd like to go there."

"You're sure?"

"I'm sure."

He reached over and squeezed her hand. "I know it's been tough these last few months, Sammy, but things will start getting better. I've already talked to Townsend and given him two weeks' notice."

"What did he say?"

"He was disappointed, but he knows how things are between Brad and me." Mr. McLean shrugged. "He wished us well."

"Did you tell him you were taking a job at Mike's?" Samantha asked. "Was he upset?"

"I did tell him, and surprisingly, he wasn't upset. He knows I want to stay in the area."

"So we're moving in two weeks," Samantha said, thinking that she'd have to concentrate all her energies on Pride's training. After they moved, she knew she'd have to give up being his groom. On the mornings when she went to Townsend Acres with Ashleigh, there would only be time to ride him in his workouts. But at least she'd see him.

When they arrived at Townsend Acres, her father parked by their apartment, and Samantha hurried inside to change. Then she headed out to the stables to tell Charlie the news. But as she was crossing the stable yard, she saw Myron Yeakel and Mr. Townsend coming out of Mr. Townsend's office. Samantha stopped in her tracks and watched as they headed toward Mr. Townsend's four-wheel-drive van. They both got in, and the van headed down the drive toward the Townsends' house, farther up on the hill.

With a hollow feeling in her stomach, she went into Pride's stable building. Hank and Charlie were inside, talking over the next day's schedule.

"Did they come in to see Pride?" she asked tightly.

Hank and Charlie seemed to understand her cryptic question. "Brad and Yeakel were in here about an hour ago," Hank said. "They took a look at the colt, then Townsend showed up, and they all went off to his office. I couldn't hear what they said, but Townsend looked like he was in darned good spirits for a change."

"Do you think it means Mr. Townsend's decided to sell?"

Charlie pursed his lips. "Who can guess what's going on around here? Townsend hasn't said anything to me, and I haven't seen Ashleigh. Since he's waited *this* long, you'd think he would hold on for another month until the colt starts racing."

Samantha swallowed back the lump in her throat. She reminded herself that the last time Yeakel had visited Pride's stall, she had jumped to the wrong conclusion. But this was Yeakel's third visit! She didn't like the odds.

Then she remembered why she'd come to see Charlie. "My father's decided to take the job at Mike's," she told him.

Charlie scowled. "Can't say I'm surprised. It's probably the best move, though it'll be a shame to lose him here."

"Maddock will be disappointed," Hank said. "But most of us figured he'd go. This isn't the best place to work anymore."

"I wonder sometimes if it's time to pack my own bags," Charlie added gruffly.

"Then who would help Ashleigh train Pride?" Samantha said.

"I didn't say I was going anywhere yet," Charlie answered. "That colt makes up for a lot of the bad stuff that goes on around here. We'll see." He narrowed his eyes and peered thoughtfully into the distance, then he looked back at Samantha. "Why don't you take him for a walk? Beautiful afternoon, and he could use a little time out of his stall."

Samantha nodded. She had planned to take Pride out anyway. "You'll tell me if you hear anything?" she said to Charlie and Hank.

"Yup. Will do."

Samantha went down the aisle and around to Pride's stall. He whickered when he saw her and came right up to the door. "Hi, big guy," Samantha said, reaching for the lead shank hanging outside the door. Pride pricked his ears and huffed in excitement. He knew what the lead shank meant. Samantha opened the door, clipped the shank to his halter, and started leading him out.

Since it was a warm spring afternoon, several grooms were out in the yard. They waved as Samantha and Pride passed. She led Pride toward the tree-canopied galloping lane. The grass underfoot had grown lush now that they were approaching the first of May. Overhead the new leaves were a paler, more fragile color. The air rang with the call of nesting birds and smelled sweetly of earth and new growth. Goddess would be racing that week-end, in her first race since the Breeders' Cup. Samantha hadn't seen the filly's last weeks of training, but Ashleigh had high hopes for her. And in another month, if everything else went well, Pride would be entered in his maiden race. Samantha felt a flutter of excitement thinking about it, then a touch of fear when she remembered Yeakel's visit.

She walked the colt up to the end of the grassy lane, then turned to head back to the stables. Pride lifted his feet high as he walked beside her, and he turned his head curiously to watch everything that was going on. Samantha's eyes welled up with tears as she watched him. She really loved the beautiful colt. And she would miss him terribly if he were moved away!

As they neared the stables, Ashleigh strode across the yard toward them. She was smiling. "Mike told me your father's taking the job," she said. "I'm so glad, Sammy."

"I'm glad too. Though I'm sure going to miss being around him all the time," she said sadly as she patted Pride.

"I know you are, but like I said, I can drive you over practically every morning. Goddess has been doing so well in training that I feel comfortable leaving her in Mike's hands."

"Did Charlie tell you Myron Yeakel was here again today?"

Ashleigh frowned. "I haven't seen Charlie yet—

and no, I wasn't told. What did he want?"

"He and Mr. Townsend were leaving when I saw them. Hank and Charlie said he looked at Pride again."

"I don't like it," Ashleigh said, shaking her head. "But Mr. Townsend promised to let me know as soon as he made a decision."

When they reached the stable yard, Samantha motioned toward Townsend's office. "There he is now," she said, feeling her stomach tighten.

Mr. Townsend quickly walked up to them. "Ashleigh, I need to talk to you," he said. "I have some news. As you know, I've been trying to work out a financial deal, and I found out this morning that it's gone through. So I won't need to sell my interest in Wonder and the colt," he said with genuine relief.

"But I heard Mr. Yeakel—" Ashleigh began.

"He came to persuade me to sell," Mr. Townsend explained. "Needless to say, he wasn't successful. Things will still be tight, but this fella doesn't have long to go before he races. I have high hopes for him, as I'm sure you do."

Samantha's knees felt shaky. Pride would be staying at Townsend Acres! A slow, happy smile spread across her face.

Ashleigh was beaming. "You know I do! And so does Sammy. He's been training incredibly well. Oh, I was so afraid that if you did sell, all that would be interrupted—"

"Well, Yeakel definitely had some plans for him," Townsend admitted. "He wanted to base him in New York and put the colt in the hands of his top trainer. Though, of course, you would have had something to say about it."

Ashleigh smiled wryly. "I doubt he would have listened."

"Which makes me even happier that the colt stays here. You and Charlie can keep him right on schedule, and we'll keep our fingers crossed. By the way, Sammy, I was sorry to hear your father's decision." He frowned. "But I understand."

"I'll miss Townsend Acres," Samantha said.

He nodded. "You're welcome to come by anytime you like."

As he strode off, the two girls turned and hugged each other excitedly.

"All right!" Ashleigh cried. "I've been waiting so long for his answer, I almost don't believe it! It's going to be tough at times, especially with you moving in two weeks—but we'll manage."

Samantha looked up at Pride. "Yes, we will."

For her remaining two weeks at the farm, Samantha spent all of her extra time with Pride, lavishing attention on him. She knew how much she was going to miss her after-school visits with him. But his future was certain now, and that was most important. She could still ride him in his workouts each morning, and at Whitebrook

181

she would be reunited with Goddess.

Charlie had Samantha breeze Pride over longer distances during the next week, and the colt loved it. Ashleigh was in heaven because Goddess had won her weekend race, and Pride's progress made her even happier. They decided on a race at Churchill Downs in Louisville for Pride, which would take place at the end of May. It would be a maiden allowance race at six furlongs, three quarters of a mile—a good starting distance for a young, still-inexperienced horse. And gradually they'd race him over longer distances. Pride was showing all the signs of wanting to run at the longer distances of a mile and a sixteenth and a mile and a quarter, and Samantha was thrilled. Those were the races in which fame and big purses could be earned.

The only one who didn't seem thrilled with Pride's progress was Brad. He watched the workouts with a scowl.

"He's miffed because he wants me and Ashleigh out of it," Charlie told Samantha when she mentioned Brad's attitude. "He'd be acting differently if he were in charge of the training."

"And he'd probably ruin Pride."

"Maybe not ruin him. The colt's got the heart and courage to win no matter what, but he'd probably try to push him too hard."

"I'm still afraid Brad's going to try to interfere," Samantha said. "I mean, it's going to be hard for

Ashleigh to spend a lot of time over here, and I'll be gone."

Charlie nodded. "It would be better all around if Townsend would let Ashleigh bring the colt over to Mike's, but I can't see that happening."

On the morning they were to move out, Samantha spent her last hour with Pride. Mike had lent the McLeans his pickup truck during the week and Samantha and her father had moved some of their things, so they only had to drive over their car, which was packed with the last of their belongings. Yvonne had come over to help, and now she stood in Pride's stall with Samantha.

"You'll still see him every day," Yvonne consoled, "and you know Hank will take good care of him."

"I know," Samantha said, hugging Pride's head, "but I wonder what he's going to think when I don't show up to see him this afternoon."

"I'll bet Charlie will be here visiting him."

Samantha smiled. "Yes. I'm pretty sure he will be. Pride has plenty of people who think he's special," she said, trying to make herself feel better. It wasn't working, though, and she blinked hot tears from her eyes. "I'll see you in the morning, boy," she whispered to the colt. "It's going to be okay."

Pride whickered and gently blew a breath against her cheek.

"Let's go," Samantha said, turning to walk down

the barn aisle. She knew she had to leave quickly or she'd start sobbing. Yvonne didn't say a word as they crossed the yard to the car, where Samantha's father was waiting. He'd said his good-byes to the staff, but Samantha had decided she wouldn't do any of that. It was the only way she could leave without breaking down, and she'd be at the farm again with Ashleigh in the morning.

"All set?" Mr. McLean said quietly as the two girls reached the car.

Samantha nodded, and she and Yvonne climbed in. No one had much to say as they drove through the countryside to Mike's, but as soon as they arrived at Whitebrook Samantha started to feel a little bit better.

Mike and his father hurried out of the house. "Glad to have you here," Mr. Reese said, shaking Mr. McLean's hand. "We'll help you get the rest of your things unpacked, and we'd like you to join us for supper tonight. I'm sure Ashleigh's coming over."

Mike grinned. "She is. Here, let me give you a hand with those bags."

Len arrived too, offering his help, and soon the car was unpacked and Samantha's father was pouring coffee for the men in the cheerful and cozy kitchen of the McLeans' new cottage. Samantha and her father had stocked the refrigerator the day before, and she got out sodas for herself and Yvonne.

As the Reeses and Mr. McLean discussed his new duties, Yvonne leaned back in her chair and smiled at Samantha. "This is nice," she said. "Much bigger than your apartment."

"It is nice," Samantha agreed. She'd given Yvonne a tour of the four-room cottage. There were two bedrooms and a bath upstairs, and a living room and kitchen downstairs to either side of the front hall.

"And you're closer to school and to my house," Yvonne added.

But farther away from Pride, Samantha thought. She shook her head, willing herself not to get depressed. She had just moved from the first place that had really felt like home, but it could have been a lot worse. She and her father could have ended up in a strange city, and Samantha could have had to attend a new school where she didn't know anyone. She looked across the table at the smiling faces of Mike and his father and sighed. No, this was much better.

15

"THE COLT'S UPSET," CHARLIE SAID GRIMLY A WEEK LATER. "Too many changes around here. He's not settling down." The old trainer leaned against the rail of the oval and scowled at Ashleigh and Samantha. "You could see that from the workout this morning. And we've only got a little over a week till his race."

Samantha had noticed the change in Pride over the last few days. He was skittish and not concentrating. She had managed to calm him down a little once they were on the track, but he hadn't put in a good performance. "What's wrong? What happened?" she asked anxiously.

"Well, for starters, he sure misses you," Charlie said, "and we lost another training groom last week—he wasn't getting along with Brad—so

Hank hasn't been able to give the colt much attention. I do what I can, but it's not enough." Charlie took off his hat and crushed it in his hand in disgust. "This place is going to rack and ruin."

Samantha laid her hand on Pride's neck. The colt was fidgeting, and his neck was damp with sweat even though she hadn't worked him that hard.

"I don't know what else we can do," Ashleigh said with a groan. "Sammy and I are already beat. We've been up before five every morning so I can pick her up and get here in time. We could try to get over more in the afternoon, but I've got finals—"

Mr. Townsend walked over as Ashleigh was speaking. He didn't look happy. "What's going on, Charlie? What's happened to him? That's three bad workouts in a row. The colt looks like he's falling to pieces."

"He is," Charlie said. "He's a sensitive animal, and he's reacting to what's going on—all the changes."

Mr. Townsend scowled. "That can't be it. I know we're shorthanded, but he's certainly not neglected. Maybe if you tried something different . . . got after him a little more. I know you're opposed to hard handling, and so am I, but the sting of a whip might get him on his toes again."

Charlie was shaking his head. "That's not the answer. If you want my advice, I'd suggest you ship him over to the Reese place."

Samantha's eyes widened as she looked over at Charlie. Mr. Townsend's tone was clipped when he responded. "Ashleigh's already suggested that to me, and I don't see the reason for it. What difference could it make?"

"First of all, it would be easier on Ashleigh and Sammy."

"We've got staff here to give a hand if it's too much of a burden," Mr. Townsend argued. "We have other riders."

"That would only unsettle him more," Charlie said. "Look, the colt's used to having Sammy around all the time. Now that he's got a new groom, his schedule's changed. Move him to the Reeses' and Sammy can start grooming him again. Ashleigh's there every day to see to his training, and I can get over from time to time. I'm not saying there's any guarantee, but the colt's got too much promise to have him fritter it away in nerves."

Townsend frowned and rubbed his chin. "You think it will make the difference between him winning and losing?"

"It'll make the difference between him settling down or not," Charlie said bluntly.

Samantha looked back and forth between the two men. She had known Ashleigh had talked to Mr. Townsend about moving Pride, but Ashleigh hadn't wanted to push Townsend too far. To hear Charlie arguing their case amazed Samantha. He didn't like to meddle and usually kept his thoughts to himself. She crossed her fingers behind her back.

Mr. Townsend's mouth was tight. "I don't like it," he said finally.

Charlie shrugged. "Up to you if you want to take a chance on wasting the best colt to come around in a long time."

Townsend's eyes swept over Pride. Then he looked to Ashleigh and Samantha. He heaved a sigh. "Okay. We'll move him, but I'll be over there to watch him work. I just hope you've got this right, Charlie."

Samantha and Ashleigh exchanged a look of disbelief. Pride was coming to Whitebrook!

On the last Saturday in May, Samantha gazed around at the crowd on the backside of Churchill Downs from her post outside Pride's stall. There was less than an hour until the first race began, and Samantha had expected a fairly large turnout. What she hadn't expected was the interest in Pride. After all, this was his maiden race, and he hadn't yet proved himself. But word had spread rapidly that Wonder's first foal was making his debut, so Samantha, Ashleigh, Charlie, Mike, and Mr. McLean took turns standing guard to keep the curious away from Pride's stall. They didn't want the noise upsetting him.

"They're expecting so much of him," Samantha said to Ashleigh. "I mean, we know how good he is, but you've only worked him on the track here once. All his clockings were at Whitebrook."

"There aren't too many secrets in racing," Ashleigh said. "And a lot of people just want to know if Wonder's son will be as good as she was."

Yvonne returned from the backside restaurant with a bag of sandwiches and drinks. She was bubbling with excitement. "I love this. Look at all the people and horses! How is he?"

"Fine," Samantha said. "I closed the stall door so he could rest. Charlie will take him up to the receiving barn in a few minutes. Mike and my father went to take a look at the rest of the field."

Charlie and Mr. Townsend walked up as Samantha reached in the bag for a sandwich, then changed her mind. Her stomach was jumping around so much, she'd probably get sick if she ate.

"Does he seem pretty settled, Sammy?" Mr. Townsend asked worriedly.

"So far, so good, though I don't know how he'll react to the crowd around the saddling paddock."

"Well, I'm certainly glad I took your advice, Charlie. He's gotten back on his toes since we moved him."

"Yup, he has," Charlie answered. "Calmed right down."

"I'd say we have a good chance of winning." From the tension on Mr. Townsend's face, Samantha could see that winning was important to him. It was important to her, too. This was the day she had been dreaming of for months, but seeing Pride put in a good performance was just as important.

"Always hard to predict a first race," Charlie said. "He's not used to crowds or running in a big field. It's better not to expect too much, just hope for a clean trip and a good effort."

Townsend nodded, but he seemed distracted. Samantha could sympathize. She was getting so nervous, she could barely think straight.

"Well, time to take him up," Charlie said. Samantha rose quickly to unlatch the stall door. Pride snorted sleepily, but immediately perked up as she led him outside. His nostrils widened, and he lifted his head as he inspected the commotion on the backside. "Just take it easy, big boy," she told him softly. "It's all new to you, but I know you'll run a good race."

Pride bobbed his head as Mr. Townsend gave him a firm pat on the shoulder. "I'll see you both in the saddling paddock."

Samantha watched as Charlie led Pride off toward the receiving barn. The colt was moving gracefully along, neck arched and copper coat shining under the green-and-gold sheet emblazoned with *Townsend Acres* covering his back. All eyes were on Pride as Charlie led him through the throngs of people, and Samantha knew she wasn't the only one admiring him.

"Seeing Charlie lead him off reminds me of Wonder racing," Ashleigh said with a little choke in her voice. "They look so much alike—and I know he'll do just as well."

Samantha nodded absently as she continued to watch the beautiful colt move off and disappear.

"Well, I'd better go change into my silks," Ashleigh said.

"And I've got to change into clean jeans for the walking ring," Samantha said. "Come on, Yvonne." Samantha grabbed her duffel bag and headed toward one of the bathrooms.

Twenty minutes later Samantha was ready, and she was hurrying to meet Charlie so that she could lead Pride into the saddling paddock with the rest of the field.

"Good luck," she heard someone say.

She turned. "Oh, hi, Tor," she said, smiling warmly. "What are you doing here?"

He grinned. "I was riding in a show here in Louisville, and I knew Pride would be running, so I thought I'd come watch. See what horse racing's all about. I hope you win."

"Thanks." Samantha smiled. "So do I."

"I'm glad things worked out okay for you," he said. "I know the last few months have been rotten. I'll be cheering. If I don't see you after the race, I'll see you in school next week."

"Right, and thanks again, Tor," Samantha said.

That was nice of him, she thought as she continued shouldering her way through the crowd. Then she saw the horses for the third race approaching down the lane from the receiving barn and quickly went over to meet Charlie.

Pride was alert and eager, and was prancing along with springing steps. Samantha took the lead attached to one side of his halter while Charlie held the other, and they proceeded toward the saddling area and walking ring behind the grandstands.

"He looks good," she said to Charlie.

"Yup. He's set and he doesn't seem to be overexcited." Charlie nodded to several racing people he knew in the crowd, and then they were entering the saddling area. Samantha's father, Mike, and Yvonne waved to them. They'd found a spot close to the edge of the walking ring and didn't look ready to budge, despite the crowd pushing in behind. Charlie and Samantha led Pride into the saddling box, and Samantha held his head while Charlie began tacking him up. Pride would be starting from post position number one.

Charlie tightened the girth and dropped the saddlecloth and flap back in place.

"Trouble with a field like this," Charlie said, adjusting his hat to keep the sun away from his eyes, "is that they've got no record. All maidens. Don't know what they'll do when they actually get out there. I watched the first two races on the monitor, though, and I don't think the rail is a bad place to be today. Okay, walk him around. He doesn't want to be standing here."

193

Pride boiled with energy. His ears were pricked, and he snorted at the new sights surrounding him. Samantha led him out around the ring. She knew they were drawing attention from the crowd. He was the son of Ashleigh's Wonder, champion filly and Horse of the Year. But rather than look at the spectators, Samantha studied the rest of the field. They were all colts and all just starting out. She couldn't deny that there were some very nice-looking horses in the field, although she was convinced Pride stood out from the others with his already magnificent build and height and the elegant carriage of his head. But she knew that beauty and conformation didn't necessarily win races. Courage and ability won, and Pride had those qualities too.

There was one other chestnut in the field, though his coat was a shade darker than Pride's. Then her eye caught on a light bay with the number five on his saddlecloth. His name was Ultrasound, a colt with incredible breeding—sired by Seattle Slew, a Triple Crown winner—and she'd read in the *Racing Form* that the handicappers were giving him a good shot.

"I think that's your competition, Pride." Samantha told him. "That guy over there. But you can beat him. You'll beat them all."

Pride responded to her voice by turning his head and playfully lipping her hair.

"No playing out there today," she warned. "But you never do, I know, once you're on the track."

The jockeys were approaching the walking ring. Mr. Townsend joined Charlie and Ashleigh as they walked over to Pride and Samantha. Ashleigh looked a little pale with nerves, and Samantha's hands were cold with sweat. She wanted so badly for Pride to show the world how great he was—to show them why she believed in him so much. It had been an awful few months, ever since Mr. Townsend had told them he might sell his interest in Pride. "If you win today, boy," Samantha murmured to the colt, "none of that bad stuff will matter to me. You'll stay at Whitebrook, and we'll keep working together."

Pride whickered deep in his throat, understanding the emotion in her voice, if not the words themselves. Then Ashleigh arrived at Samantha's side and gave her hand a squeeze. "We're going to do it, Sammy."

Samantha returned the squeeze. "I know we are."

But as Charlie gave Ashleigh a leg into the saddle and relayed his last-minute thoughts on strategy in the race, Samantha's stomach started flopping. It didn't help to hear Mr. Townsend say almost grimly, "We need this one for the farm."

What if Pride didn't win? What if he hated being out on a real track, with horses and jockeys jostling him, with dirt flying in his face, with crowds roaring? What if he didn't even put in a good effort?

Samantha shook her head. She couldn't think of that. He *would* put in a good effort. She took Pride's head in her hands and dropped a good-luck kiss on his nose. "You're going to make everybody proud, big guy. I know it."

He whickered affectionately, then Ashleigh and Pride were heading out of the walking ring toward the tunnel under the grandstand that led to the track. Samantha watched them until they were out of sight. "I know you can do it, Pride," she whispered.

Samantha and her father, Yvonne, and Mike bustled over to the grandstand while Mr. Townsend went off to his reserved clubhouse seats. He'd urged Charlie to join him since the old trainer was Pride's co-trainer, but Charlie had muttered, "Don't like all that highfalutin stuff. We've got decent enough seats. If he wins, we'll see you down below."

Samantha sat gripping her knees as she watched the field warm up. Their seats were high in the grandstand, and they had a sweeping view of the track. She studied every horse in the field, looking for signs of overexcitement, unruliness, or lethargy. She lifted her binoculars for a closer look. Pride did seem to be handling it all the best. He was energetic and just a little feisty, but there was no lathered sweat on his neck, and he seemed to be minding his rider. Ultrasound, unfortunately, looked cool and determined too.

196

Samantha turned her binoculars to Ashleigh. It was difficult to see much from so far away, but Ashleigh's face looked tense as she and Pride loaded into the chute in the gate positioned off the backstretch. "You can do it, guys. I know you can!" Samantha whispered.

Once the other horses were loaded, the gate doors snapped open. "And they're off!" came the booming voice of the announcer. "Wonder's Pride has broken cleanly, Ultrasound coming up through the middle . . . Believeitornot making a strong bid on the outside . . . then Watkins Glen, Shirfall . . . "

Samantha watched Pride as he surged along the inside rail. Then her breath caught in her throat. It looked like he'd been bumped—badly—by the horse outside of him. She heard Charlie mutter under his breath. And Pride had certainly reacted from the impact. His ears pricked in surprise and he lost concentration.

Samantha tried to think of what she would do if she were in his saddle—gently twitch on the reins to get his attention, talk to him—and Ashleigh seemed to be doing the same. In the next instant, he was in gear again. He shot through a narrow gap on the rail. His ears were pitched back, listening, waiting for his rider's commands, but Samantha could see that he was striving on his own. He wanted to get back in the fight. He surged forward, away from the colt who'd bumped him. Ultrasound and Believeitornot had gotten a length lead

197

on him, but both of them were running wide, out close to the middle of the track. Samantha saw Ashleigh point Pride and set him down. It was such a short race—only six furlongs. Every jockey maneuver counted. Then Pride came roaring up along the rail.

"Wonder's Pride is eating up their lead!" the announcer shouted. "They've left an opening, and he's coming through. This colt has found another gear—and he's blowing them away!"

Samantha watched in breathless ecstasy as Pride pounded up the rail. He was moving so fast, the other horses looked like they were standing still. He was incredible—absolutely incredible!

"All right!" Yvonne screamed. "Go, Pride!"

"He's going . . . going . . . he is gone!" the announcer screeched. "Six lengths! A six-length victory for the son of Ashleigh's Wonder . . . *despite* a troubled trip. I think we're looking at something here!"

"We are!" Samantha cried, throwing her arms in the air. "He did it!" She turned around to hug Yvonne, who was jumping up and down in excitement. Mr. McLean and Mike were laughing.

"What a race! Wow, he showed them!" yelled Mike.

Charlie took the rumpled hat he'd been holding, shook out the creases, and put it back on his head. "Yup. He showed what he's got."

"And there'll be more to come!" Samantha thrust

198

her fist in the air. "Watch out, world!" She looked down to the track, where Ashleigh was heading toward the winner's circle. Pride's neck was arched and his step was springy. He seemed to be enjoying his first taste of glory. Samantha blew him a well-deserved kiss. His victory was better than she'd even dreamed, and she sure had reason to dream now.

"Well," Charlie said gruffly, interrupting her reverie. "What are you waiting for? You've got a horse in the winner's circle."

Yes, she sure did!

📚 HarperPaperbacks *By Mail*

Read all the books in the
THOROUGHBRED series!

#1 A Horse Called Wonder—Is Ashleigh's love enough to save a sick foal?

#2 Wonder's Promise—Has bad training ruined Wonder forever?

#3 Wonder's First Race—Is Wonder's racing career over before it begins?

#4 Wonder's Victory—At last—all of Ashleigh's dreams have come true. But will she and Wonder be separated forever?

And don't miss these other great books by *Thoroughbred* author Joanna Campbell:

Battlecry Forever!
Everyone says that Battlecry is a loser who will never race again. Leslie is determined to prove them all wrong. But will Battlecry let *her* down, too?

Star of Shadowbrook Farm
After a bad fall, Susan has sworn never to ride again. Then Evening Star comes into her life. He needs her to help make him a winner, but can she overcome her fears?

MAIL TO: Harper Collins Publishers
P.O.Box 588, Dunmore, PA 18512-0588

TELEPHONE: 1-800-331-3716 (Visa and Mastercard holders!)
YES, please send me the following titles:

Thoroughbred
❏ #1 A Horse Called Wonder (0-06-106120-4) $3.50
❏ #2 Wonder's Promise (0-06-106085-2) $3.50
❏ #3 Wonder's First Race (0-06-106082-8) $3.50
❏ #4 Wonder's Victory (0-06-106083-6) $3.50

❏ Battlecry Forever! (0-06-106771-7) $3.50
❏ Star of Shadowbrook Farm (0-06-106783-0) $3.50

SUBTOTAL..$_____
POSTAGE AND HANDLING* ....$ 2.00
SALES TAX (Add applicable state sales tax) ....$_____
                            TOTAL: ....$_____
                    (Remit in U.S. funds. Do not send cash.)

NAME_____
ADDRESS_____
CITY_____
STATE_____ ZIP _____

Allow up to six weeks for delivery. Prices subject to change. Valid only in U.S. and Canada.

*Free postage/handling if you buy four or more!   H0431